DAY TRIPS

A COLLECTION OF SHORT FICTION

SIDEWALK LABS

SIDEWALK LABS

U.S.A.

First edition. May 2014.

Cover art by Yuliana Butchko

ISBN 978-0692212264

Thoughts

by C.K. Adams

Larry watched Flora from where he was standing by the sink, thinking, She's doing it again; I don't know how to handle this.

What she was doing was acting weird, not in any particular way he could say, but she was definitely becoming unpredictable, sometimes flat-out strange. Sometimes scary. She was about to do something, he didn't know what, but she had stopped for no reason in the hallway and her face was starting to contort in unusual ways. He tried to tell what to expect from her face – a screaming fit? Hysterical sobbing? Or just fifteen more minutes of standing there, in the hallway, making strange expressions.

Insane expressions, he thought.

She seemed to break out of it at that moment, and looked his way. He avoided her gaze and went back to moving dishes from the sink to the dishwasher. She came into the kitchen, walking behind him to the refrigerator.

"I have a toothache," she said.

"Is it bad?" he asked, not turning around. "You think I should call the dentist?" Relieved, thinking, maybe this wasn't an episode, after all.

"Maybe," she said. Still with the refrigerator open. "I think—" she stopped, and he turned around, watched her lift the milk out and onto the counter. "I think maybe I'm picking up the radio or something, in my mouth."

"What, in your teeth?" Larry said.

"Yeah, maybe," she said, uncapping the milk. "In my fillings."

"You have fillings?" he said. He hadn't known.

"You know that," she said. He shrugged. "Silver," she said.

"I don't think you can pick up the radio from silver fillings," he said, "I saw that on Mythbusters."

"Well what do they know?" she said. She sounded irritated.

"I can call the dentist," he said.

"Yeah," she said. She recapped the milk and put it back in the refrigerator. She hadn't used it, he noticed. She's gone strange, he thought, shaking his head.

*****

Flora went from the kitchen to the bathroom, thinking, maybe I could use something to pry my fillings out. She had two, one on each side, top row, towards the back. Might only need to pry the left one out, she thought, which was the ear the radio was playing on. The right ear was fine, hunky-dory.

She found the constant, tinny drone in one ear aggravating. Might be better, she thought, if it *was* playing in both ears. Like wearing headphones. Might be better, she thought, if I could at least choose the station. Right now it was tuned into some bullshit Christian evangelist.

Flora didn't like the whiny way his voice sounded.

In the medicine cabinet she found her big pair of tweezers. When she picked them up, the radio voice started to cut in and out, and she got the idea that maybe the tweezers were acting like a radio antenna. She held them over her head, moving them very slowly back and forth. Eventually she found a spot where, if she stayed perfectly still, the radio voice just turned into static.

Blessed static. She held her arm like that until it got too tired and wobbled and the radio voice cut back in. "And the cock crowed," said the whiny voice, solemnly. "To realize," the voice said, through bits of static, "that moment of your own betrayal."

Flora pounded the counter with her fist until she saw herself in the mirror (*do I really look that crazy?*) and took a deep breath and wiped her hands on her jeans. She ran the sink and splashed some water on her face. She opened her mouth and leaned her head back, looking at the reflection of her fillings, two dark shadows in the back of her mouth.

At first she couldn't get the tweezers to fit comfortably between her teeth. She had to pull them apart until they bent opposite directions, which wasn't easy. Then she stabbed the pointy end of one side into the filling on the left, trying to pry under an edge. It hurt a lot and it felt like she was getting tiny metal shavings on her tongue, but it didn't seem like she was making progress working the silver loose. The pain was starting to make her cry.

She gave that up and went back to waving her now bent tweezer antenna in the air. Eventually, she found two more beautiful minutes of quiet meditation. Enough for her to believe she could ignore it a while longer, at least until Larry called the dentist.

*****

In the waiting room at the dentist, two days later, Larry nudged Flora gently when she started to snore.

"Honey," he whispered, but she just made an irritated face in her sleep and kept snoring. There were a few other people in the waiting room, including one little boy that was staring at Flora. Larry frowned at the boy. The boy frowned back. Larry nudged Flora again, embarrassed. "Honey, wake up," he said.

"Fine," said Flora, opening her eyes. "Fine, I'm awake." She sounded like she resented it.

"Sorry," Larry mumbled.

"It's fine," said Flora, while in her left ear she listened to a radio talk show on books. It could be a lot more terrible than that, she thought. It could be that radio evangelist, which was who she seemed to pick up the most. To combat the constant signal, she had taken to sleeping a lot. Over the past two days she had slept over thirty hours, and here she was again, falling asleep in the waiting room. She knew Larry was embarrassed, but she didn't care. Sleep was wonderful. She was falling in love with sleep and Larry could go to hell.

"Have you ever read *Pan's Pain*," she asked Larry.

He shrugged. "No, never heard of it."

"It's a national bestseller," she said.

"Yeah?" Larry wasn't much of a reader.

"I hear it's compelling, though the symbolism might be a bit heavy-handed." said Flora. "I've never read it either, but it sounds interesting." Larry didn't say anything. "I wish he'd hurry," said Flora, referring to the dentist.

"Yeah," said Larry. He was trying to ignore the little boy who was making faces at him.

"I don't think that kid likes you," said Flora.

"I don't like *him*," said Larry.

The radio in Flora's ear changed briefly to static, then, to Flora's dismay, to the whiny-voiced Christian evangelist who she seemed to pick up far too often. My fillings must be tuned to their frequency, she thought. "This is taking an awfully damn long time," she said, irritably. "What time is it?"

Larry looked at his watch. "3:42." Flora was right, it was taking a very long time. "I don't think I like our dentist much," he said. "This *is* a bit inconsiderate."

"A bit!" repeated Flora.

"And he was a little rude to me on the phone, I thought," he said, lowering his voice. "All I did was, I told the receptionist you wanted your fillings removed. She put me on hold. Next thing you know our dentist comes on and starts yelling at me."

"Like, shouting?" said Flora. But when he started to answer, she interrupted him: "Here, switch places with me." It was making her nuts trying to listen to him with her left ear, with the fool preacher going on and on.

"What?" said Larry, not understanding, but he dutifully got up and let her move into his seat. "Anyway," he said, "he wasn't exactly yelling, but he was being very abrasive."

"What did he say?"

"Don't exactly remember," Larry shrugged. "Something about mercury poisoning."

"Did you tell him about the radio?"

"I didn't really get the chance," he said. "Well, I did tell him," he amended, "but I don't think he was listening."

"But he's going to remove them?" she demanded.

"Well," Larry said, "that's what I told him you wanted. And he said come in at 2:30."

"He's going to remove them," Flora said. She sounded determined.

"That's what I told him on the phone," said Larry.

I shall read for you, said the radio preacher, *this passage from the Holy Book: "Therefore, says the Lord, I will be silent no longer concerning their ungodly acts, neither will I tolerate their wicked practices."*

You are cruel, God, she thought. Torturing sadist. "He's mocking me," she said aloud.

"Who?" said Larry, "That kid?"

"No," said Flora. "Never mind."

*****

"We were kept waiting a very long time," said Flora to the dentist, Dr. Eckenhammer.

"I'm a very busy man," Eckenhammer said, without apology. He looked at the chart he had in his hand. "It says here you want fillings removed?"

"Yes, I'm getting—"

"*Silver* fillings, it says here."

"Yes, they're—"

"No doubt you're concerned about the mercury." He was frowning, and – Flora would swear to it – *sneering* at her.

"Mercury?" Flora said.

Eckenhammer sniffed dramatically. "I know why you're here, you've read the articles in the magazine, you're disturbed about the amalgam, the slow mercury poisoning. Don't be so foolish!" He glared. "It's hype. It's propaganda. You are much more at risk by *removing* the amalgam fillings, releasing the mercury into the system. You might as well not do it. I don't care what your *Cosmo* or your *Woman's Day* said, your fillings are not dangerous."

Flora stared at him. "I don't read magazines," she said stiffly. "I'm here because I'm picking up the radio in my silver fillings, and that's why you're going to remove them today."

"They're not silver. Well, some. Also zinc, copper, tin. Mercury." His head cocked to the side. "The radio, you say? A particular station?"

"Christian talk. Sometimes rock. Sometimes," —she made a face— "country."

"Frequency?" he said.

"All the time," she said. "Please, I'm begging. Take them out."

"I mean, radio frequency? Call letters? Band?" He had wheeled closer and was shining a big light in her face. "What's the station?"

"I don't know," she said, "how the hell am I supposed to know?"

"Commercials?" he said. "Advertisements? Call-this-number-now?"

"No," she said, shaking her head. "Nothing like that."

He looked at her. "A radio station with no commercials?" He sounded skeptical.

"I don't know," she said, frustrated. "Maybe it's that new XM satellite radio."

"I don't think," he said, "that it's possible to pick up a radio station in your fillings. Most especially satellite radio." But he seemed less stern and more curious. "You're hearing something right now?"

"Yes," she said. "Always. All the damn time! You've got to take them out."

"I've been trying to explain, Mrs." —he looked at the chart— "Stewart-Madison," "it's not an entirely safe procedure to remove the fillings. There's the moderate danger of mercury poisoning. Silver fillings are fifty percent mercury, which you know, of course, is highly toxic."

"I did know," she said.

"Standard safety procedures are not adequate. It requires preparation."

"Well," Flora said, "I hope you're prepared."

"We will not be able to remove your fillings today," Eckenhammer said.

"Yes, we will," said Flora, adamantly.

"It cannot be done," said Eckenhammer.

"It can," Flora insisted.

"I have, however," Eckenhammer said, "a possible solution, of my own devising. A temporary solution, until our next appointment, when I have prepared my office a bit better for your filling removal. What I believe I can do today is coat the fillings with a thin copper layer, perfectly safe, of course, which should interrupt the reception of the radio signals. Possibly, this will alleviate the problem entirely."

"Possibly," repeated Flora, not liking the sound of that.

"If not, we will schedule to remove the fillings, which even after proper preparation runs some risk."

"Schedule," repeated Flora, not liking the sound of that, either.

"Mrs. Stewart-Madison, I have some doubts that the fillings are causing your problem at all. I find it extremely unlikely. Still, I am willing to try the copper coating. If radio signals are indeed the problem, it should do the trick."

"Fine," said Flora. "Just do it, please. Get it done."

"Excellent," said Eckenhammer. "Lean back all the way and open your mouth wide. Say 'aah,' please. Let me just take a look here."

*****

Larry popped a piece of chewing gum into his mouth, thinking, maybe after the fillings are removed, she'll go back to being the old Flora. Well, minus a couple fillings, and plus about thirty or forty pounds — she'd started eating like a hog ever since she started to turn crazy — most of it in her stomach, which he'd noticed had started to pooch out and sag just a bit.

I doubt the fillings will fix that, Larry thought. Those pounds might be here to stay, he thought.

He wasn't sure he believed the whole radio story, anyway. First, it didn't explain all of the little insanities she'd developed. For instance, she'd started to repeat herself several times over the course of a day. On one occasion she had told the same story, something that happened at work, *three times* over the course of dinner.

9

He had pointed it out to her, the third time. She had looked completely blank, then laughed it off, but it was obvious she had no memory of her earlier narrations.

And it didn't explain the occasional nonsense syllables that randomly appeared in her sentences. Or the tic that had developed in her left hand. Or the intent way she'd stare into open space. Or any of the other things.

"Can I sit here?" the boy from across the waiting room said, interrupting Larry's reverie. It was the kid who had been making faces at him earlier, sneaking up on him. He was indicating the seat Flora had vacated, in which he could still see the imprint of her behind.

"My wife is sitting there," he said, mashing his eyebrows down but trying not to scowl too much. He didn't much care for little kids.

"Can I have a piece of gum?" the kid said. He couldn't have been more than six or seven years old. He doesn't realize how much he's been annoying me, Larry thought. "Sure," he said, "if you go back over there and sit with your Mommy."

"That's not my Mommy," the kid said. "That's my Aunt Donna."

"You'll go back and sit with your Aunt Donna, then," said Larry.

"Yes," said the boy.

"Good," said Larry. He handed the kid a piece of gum.

"Thank you," said the boy politely, sitting down in the seat next to Larry.

"Aren't you going to go sit with your Aunt Donna?" said Larry, exasperated.

The boy shrugged. "Aunt Donna said I could sit here."

He seemed perfectly friendly, like they had broken the ice. "Said I could sit wherever I want."

"My wife's sitting there," said Larry, tightly.

"Where's she?" shrugged the boy.

"She'll be back," said Larry.

"She looked funny."

"That's not a very nice thing to say about somebody," said Larry.

"I like your dog," said the boy, pointing to the logo on Larry's shirt. "What's that say? Is that his name?" He ran his finger across the brand name: *le beagle.*

"I don't think he has a name," said Larry.

"My name's Raymond," the kid said, with pride. "What's your name?"

"Mr. Madison," said Larry.

"That's a funny name," Raymond said. "I know a lot about names. Everybody has a name."

"Is he bothering you," said Raymond's Aunt Donna, coming over.

"No, not at all," said Larry. He didn't want to seem like a mean guy. "We were talking about names."

"He's too friendly," she said.

"He's fine," said Larry. She was twenty-eight, twenty-nine. Massive knockers. He tried not to be drawn into a trance by her cleavage.

"Was that your wife," Donna said, "you're waiting on?"

Larry shrugged, then nodded, not saying anything out loud.

"Yeah," she said, and gave him a knowing smile. "I'm Donna," she said.

If Flora came out and saw him talking to this girl, Larry

thought, a girl looking like this, she'd pitch a fit. But we're just talking, thought Larry. Chatting it up. Not doing anything wrong. Besides, he figured, she'll be in there a while.

*****

When Flora came out of the dentist's office, Donna had already left. Larry had discovered she worked at the bar down the street from where he worked and had promised to drop in and see her. She had seemed fun, he thought.

"Well?" he asked Flora. "Better?"

She nodded. "Is gone," she mumbled. "My mouth is numb."

"He took out the fillings?" he said.

"No," she said. "But he fixed it."

"No more radio?"

"No more," she said. "Is gone."

*****

She woke him up in the middle of the night, crying and moaning. "What is it?" he said.

"It's back," she said. "It's worse. It's in both ears." She got out of bed and went into the bathroom. She was in there a while, and eventually Larry drifted back to sleep.

When he woke up, she still wasn't in the bed. He found her downstairs in the kitchen, eating cookies and milk.

"I heard you," she said. "Coming down the stairs."

"Oh?" he said. He got some bread out and put it in the toaster.

"I can hear everything," she said. "It's so *loud*."

"You need to go back to the dentist?" he said.

"I *hate* him!" she spat.

"I can call another one," he said.

Flora didn't respond for a moment. Then she said, "I know you think I'm fat."

"Oh?" Larry said, expressionless.

Flora said, "I know you think I eat sweets all the time." She took a deliberate bite of a cookie dripping with milk.

"Do you think you eat sweets all the time?" Larry asked.

"Bastard," she said. "I know you think I'm dumpy and irritating. You think I'm going crazy," she said accusingly.

The toast popped out and Larry started to spread peanut butter on one of the slices.

"I can hear *everything*, Larry," Flora said. "Don't you get it? I can even hear your thoughts."

She's off her rocker, Larry thought. If she could really hear my thoughts, she'd say something about my sleeping with Rachel, he thought. He thought it loudly and clearly in his head, practically daring her.

"It's so goddamn *loud*," she said.

"I'll call another dentist," Larry said.

She looked at him a long moment. "I think you're dangerous," she whispered, and left the kitchen.

*****

He sat at the table eating. He didn't notice her come back in, not until she had already started to swing and sliced a chunk out of his shoulder with one of the steak knives.

He screamed and clawed at his arm, standing up and swinging back at the same time. He caught her in the face and sent her flying toward the stove.

13

"I'm not going to let you do it!" she said. "I hear what you're planning!"

"Crazy bitch," he spat. "What the hell is wrong with you?"

"You won't kill me, you prick!" she screamed. She came at him again, the knife intended somewhere for the neck area. He grabbed her wrist and twisted it. She struggled, she kept trying to push the knife into his chest and stomach. She was surprisingly strong, and it was a hard fight with his arm screaming in pain.

He grunted and kicked her in the stomach, at the same time pushing her with his uninjured arm. She stumbled backwards, and he fell on top of her, the knife twisting in her direction. His arm pushed it forward, and the tip of the blade caught her in the collar and stabbed through the bottom of her neck. She gurgled, and her body jerked under his twice, like she was coughing.

He pushed off of her and stood up, his body shaking. "Flora?" he said, but it was obvious she was dead.

Self-defense, he thought. Clearly self-defense. Crazy bitch attacked me.

He was shivering and sweating. His stomach clenched with nausea. In the back of his throat a sound was developing.

Calm down, he thought. Self-defense. She'd gone completely off of her rocker.

Thinking *what*? he thought. Thinking she could hear people's thoughts through her fillings? Thinking she could hear *my* thoughts through her silver fillings?

Thinking what? he thought. That I thought she was fat? That I was going to kill her?

I wasn't going to kill her, he thought. His hand was still shaking as he dialed 911.

Sure, he'd thought about it. It had passed through his mind.

But he hadn't really been going to do it.

It was just a thought, he thought. That's how the mind is, he thought. There's no controlling it.

Thoughts go where they want, and there's just no stopping them.

The Road Unravels Backwards

by Curt Cannon

It so happened that once when Dorothy was again on her way to Oz, she came across the Shaggy Man standing across a road that turned sharply and disappeared around the corner. "Why look," she said to Toto, "It's the Shaggy Man. We should go and say hello." So she and Toto walked over to where her road crossed the Shaggy Man's road. "Hello, Shaggy Man," said Dorothy, and Toto nodded twice and barked once and turned around in a circle.

"Hello, Dorothy," said the Shaggy Man. "I'm sorry, I can't let you go down this road."

"Well, why not?" asked Dorothy. "It looks like a perfectly all right road to me."

"Oh, no, don't think so." The Shaggy Man shook his head vigorously. "You don't want to go down this road, surely."

"Well, what's wrong with it?"

The Shaggy Man leaned forward a bit, turning his head and whispering. "Why, it's the road that unravels backward."

"Backward?" said Dorothy, ever curious. "What does that mean?"

"Most roads go forward, don't they?" asked the Shaggy Man.

"I don't know about that," said Dorothy, who didn't imagine roads went anywhere, except there were some roads that had apparently gotten somewhere else, as she could never find them again. Roads to Oz especially were often like this. It was usually much easier to find a *new* road to Oz then one you had traveled before. "Most people do go forward on roads, though, I can tell you that."

"Of course they do," said the Shaggy Man, "Straight ahead, that's the proper way to go on a normal road. But on this road," and here his voice sunk to a whisper again, "on this road when you go forward, the road unravels backward."

"Well what if you went backward?" asked Dorothy.

"I don't know," Shaggy answered, surprised. "I never thought of that."

"Now look," said Dorothy, growing impatient, "Is that the road to Oz or not?"

The Shaggy Man gave her a slightly puzzled look. "I suppose it would take you there. But why would you want to go to Oz, where you've already been, instead of Oz, where you were going?"

Now this was too much turning about of words for Dorothy. Impatiently waving her hand, she said, "Shaggy

Man, I am on my way to Oz, and if this is the way I'm taking it. So stand aside, or I'll have Toto bark at you."

The Shaggy Man looked very frightened at this. Shaking his head at Dorothy, he slowly stepped aside, putting a few more feet between himself and the dog. Toto growled and bounced off down the backward road. "Wait, Toto, you get back here," shouted Dorothy, and she ran down the road after him, leaving the Shaggy Man behind.

A distance down the road, Dorothy caught up to Toto digging in the bushes. "Why whatever is the matter?" she marveled at Toto's excitement, as he pawed furiously at the ground. "One would think you'd seen a rabbit." Toto looked up at her, panting, and blinked once, firmly. Indeed, something was scurrying in the bushes, and Dorothy caught a quick glimpse. "Toto," she said, "that's no rabbit! What is that?" And together they hurried after it, as it scrambled away into the trees.

A few steps into the forest, Dorothy found a small man with a round stomach trying to hide behind a tree. "You!" she said. "What are you doing there? Trying to scare little girls?" The little man gave a frightened sound and ran further into the forest. "I won't hurt you!" Dorothy yelled after him. "I just want to know if this is the way to Oz."

The little man stopped and looked back at her. "What's that you say, Miss?" he said, in a high-pitched funny little voice.

"I said, is this the way to Oz?"

The man shrugged. "I don't know any Oz," he said, "but I don't think this is it."

"Are you sure?" asked Dorothy. "The Shaggy Man told me this road would get me there."

The little man shrugged again. "Don't know any Oz," he repeated. "Don't think this land has a name. It's the King's land. It's all the King's land. Don't need a name."

"Drat," said Dorothy, stamping her foot. This excited Toto, who barked and hopped a time or two. "Say," Dorothy said to the little round man, who was still looking fidgety and ready to run, "what is that you've got behind your back?" The little man gave a start. "Well?" said Dorothy, "what is it?"

Reluctantly, the little man revealed the small shovel he had been trying to hide.

"A shovel?" said Dorothy. "What are you going to do with that?"

"Dig," said the little man shortly, and turned and ran.

"Hey!" yelled Dorothy. "Wait, don't run!" She sighed, lifting her dress up around her knees and chasing into the woods after him. "Come back! Come on, Toto, let's find him!" So together they ran into the forest.

The found him a little farther along, breathing heavily, sitting on a tree stump, the shovel resting on the ground by his side. He wheezed at her.

"Well, I don't know what you had to run for," said Dorothy, reprovingly. "I could have fallen and scraped a knee, you know."

The little man grunted.

"So why do you have a shovel?" Dorothy said. "Are you not supposed to? Is that why you're running?"

"You don't know much, do you?" said the little man, between gasps.

"That's not a very nice thing to say," said Dorothy.

"Not supposed to be digging on the King's land," he

said. "Everybody knows that."

"Oh," said Dorothy. "Well, I didn't know. But if I see him, I won't tell him."

"You're very kind," said the little man.

"If I may ask," said Dorothy, "what is it you're digging for?"

At that the little man hemmed and hawed and looked around guiltily. "Just," said the man, "for no reason."

"Oh, I don't believe that for one second," said Dorothy. "It's all right, you can tell me. I won't tell anyone. And certainly Toto won't." And Toto wagged and nodded.

"My bro," mumbled the chubby fellow.

"What?" said Dorothy. "Your brother?"

"My little brother," he said.

"You're digging for your little brother?"

"Digging *up* my little brother," he clarified.

"Oh," said Dorothy, nonplussed. "Does he need digging up?"

"Yes," the little man sighed. "I came down the road one way and buried him, and now I've gone down the other way to dig him up." To Dorothy's surprise, a small tear leaked out of the corner of one eye. "He was dead, you see." He wiped the tear away and smiled unsteadily. "But now, if I've gone all the right ways, he should be all right again, once I dig him up."

"How very strange," said Dorothy. At that point they heard a sound, not very far away, and they both rushed over to where a voice was rising from the ground.

"Hello?" said the voice, weak and quavering. Toto barked furiously at the bare little patch of earth. "Hello? I hear someone," the voice said.

"It's my brother!" the little man said to Dorothy, "I've found him!" He took his shovel and started digging. "Hold on, Beanpole," he yelled at the ground, "I'm coming!"

"Squat, is that you?" the ground quavered.

"Is your name Squat?" interjected Dorothy to the little man.

"Yes!" yelled, Squat, to Dorothy and the ground. "Don't worry, Beanpole, I'm coming!" And shortly he had dug the dirt loose and a hand came free, waving in the air. Squat grabbed it, and Dorothy, wanting to be helpful, grabbed the wrist, and together they pulled.

"What a very large hand," said Dorothy, and then, as they kept pulling, "What a very long arm," and then, when they had backed up nearly seven feet and Beanpole's feet were kicking free, she said, "My, what a very tall person you are." But Beanpole ignored her, as he was leaning over to embrace his brother Squat.

"Squat," he said, wiping tears from his cheeks, "thank heavens! It felt like eternity down there."

"It's all right, little brother," said Squat.

"And thank you for your help," said Beanpole, looking down at Dorothy, "whoever you are."

"I'm Dorothy," she said, "and this is Toto," and Toto spun and raised a paw.

"Well, Dorothy," said Squat, beaming a smile, "since you were kind enough to help us, maybe we can help you. Where did you say you were going?"

"I'm looking for Oz," said Dorothy. "And I think it must be near. Or at least nearer there than Kansas," she amended, "for I know certainly people don't climb up from the ground near there."

Squat looked blank, but Beanpole said, "I've heard tell of Oz."

"Really?" said Dorothy, Toto barking.

"I think it's down the road a ways. That way," he said, pointing the direction Dorothy had been going. "Might be some distance though," he said.

"Well, I shall get there eventually," said Dorothy.

"We can walk with you a ways," said Squat. "Wouldn't do for a young girl to be walking out here alone."

"I've got Toto," said Dorothy, but Squat and Beanpole insisted, so together the four of them made their way back to the road and continued down it.

After a bit they came to a stream that crossed the road, over which no bridge appeared to be built. "Should we swim across?" Squat asked, coming over the hill, but Dorothy, who was standing next to the stream, said, "I don't think it's very deep."

Indeed, when they came up next to it, they could see it wasn't very deep at all. In some places it was just water running over rocks, or, as Beanpole put it, "Water running up the rocks. Look at it!" And he was right. Instead of falling down the rocks, the water appeared to be dripping up from rock to rock.

"How very odd!" said Dorothy. "The stream is flowing backwards."

"It's this road," said Beanpole, "the Queen's Southwesterly Highway. It's haunted."

"Yes," said Squat, "it's the ghosts that push the water the wrong way. There are hundreds of them. Sailors, I think, that drowned in the river."

"Drowned in *that* river?" said Dorothy, looking at the

inches of water.

"It used to be bigger," said Beanpole, scratching his head with a long finger.

"We shan't have any trouble crossing *that*," said Dorothy, and she picked up Toto in one hand and hooked her dress with the other and began taking delicate steps across the wet stones.

"Oh, no need for that," said Beanpole, and he picked up Dorothy and Toto in one of his long arms, and Squat in the other, and he started trudging across the stream. But a strange thing happened as they crossed: the stream seemed to get wider and deeper, and before long the water came up to Beanpole's knees. And then it was up to his waist. And after that it was as high as his chest, and he had to lift Dorothy and Squat up above his shoulders, and then they were across and Beanpole set them down onto dry land.

"Oh my!" said Dorothy, looking at them. "What's happened to you?" Something strange had certainly happened: Beanpole had gotten shorter, and Squat, somehow, had gotten thinner (though still a bit round in the middle).

"Squat, you look so young," said Beanpole, in a high voice that cracked.

"Look at you!" responded Squat. "You can't be more than fourteen."

"It must be the Fountain of Youth," said Beanpole, looking at the stream. "It's made us young."

"Can't be the Fountain of Youth," said Squat. He indicated Dorothy. "She looks like she's the same age as before."

"I don't feel any younger," said Dorothy, feeling her face with her fingers and putting her hand on her head to see how tall she was.

"Nope, you look the same," said Beanpole, his voice cracking again. "I don't want to be a teenager again," he grumbled.

"Well, how will you get older again?" said Dorothy. "Should we find a Fountain of Age?"

"Never heard of such a thing," said Squat. "Maybe we'll just have to age the normal way again." He didn't appear to mind being younger himself.

Then they heard a voice: "Cross the stream the other way."

"What?" said Dorothy. "Who said that?" She looked around but didn't see anybody else. In any case, Beanpole had already bolted back into the stream and was almost at the other side, carrying a mildly protesting Squat.

"It works," shouted Beanpole, his voice back to normal. "Dorothy, are you coming? You can come to our house for dinner!"

What a nice offer, thought Dorothy, but I must be very near Oz, as strange as things have turned. "No, but thank you," she shouted back across. "Toto and I are going to find our way to Oz."

And again she heard a voice: "Because because because because because."

"What was that?" she said, peering intently where the voice had been. Toto barked and raised a ready paw, but again they saw nothing. She waved her goodbyes to Beanpole and Squat, watching as they disappeared down the road. "That was certainly odd," she said to Toto. "I'm almost certain I heard a voice." Toto barked, shaking his tail furiously and turning in a circle. "Toto, is there someone there?" asked Dorothy. The little dog barked again, pressing close to the ground and growling at a spot in the air.

Dorothy ran to Toto and scooped him into her arms. "Toto, you're shaking," she said, tucking him under her elbow. "Whoever you are," she said angrily, into the trees, "you'd better quit scaring my dog and show yourself. It's not nice, hiding like that." She and Toto peered into the shadows.

"You won't see him if he doesn't want you to," said a voice behind them, and Dorothy spun around, startled. Standing there, on the other side of a road, was a little girl about her own age. "I'm Alice," she said.

Dorothy looked her over suspiciously. "That wasn't your voice I heard."

Alice shrugged. "I didn't say anything. It was the cat."

Toto growled and barked and growled and tried to jump out of Dorothy's arms. "Quiet, Toto," said Dorothy, holding on more firmly. She looked back into the trees. "I don't see a cat," she said. "And besides, cats don't talk." She narrowed her eyes at the other girl. "Is it your cat?"

"No," said Alice. "At least, I don't think so. It follows me." She hesitated. "I think." She pointed back into the woods. "Look, there he is!"

Dorothy looked over and saw nothing at first. Then, she made out a small shape, hanging in the air. She blinked and looked again. "Is that an eye?" she said. "It winked at me." Next another eye appeared, and then a smile. "Quiet, Toto," she said absentmindedly, as the little dog was

26

barking furiously and straining.

"See," said Alice, "it's a cat," as the whole head of a smiling cat appeared. "Talk," demanded Alice, but the cat smiled even wider, and then the face disappeared completely. "He tries to annoy me, I believe," said Alice. "What's your name?"

"Dorothy," said Dorothy. "Can you help me? I'm trying to find Oz."

"No such place," said Alice, shaking her head.

"Is too," said Dorothy. "I've been there."

"Maybe you dreamed it."

"And I must be close," said Dorothy, "as things have turned so odd."

"Oh," said Alice. "You're looking for *Odds*. I know where that is." She pointed down the road where Dorothy had been headed. "Odds is that way." She spread her hands apologetically. "I thought you said Oz."

"I *did* say Oz," said Dorothy.

"Then I can't help you. Never heard of Oz. But I *can* take you to Odds, which could be very like Oz."

"I don't have any friends in Odds," said Dorothy. "Is that where you're going?"

At that, the other girl's face fell. "No," she said shortly. "I'm not going anywhere, really." They heard a snicker from behind them, and both girls turned to see the cat's smile disappearing. Toto barked and jumped out of Dorothy's arm, circling the spot where the cat had disappeared.

"Do you have friends in Odds?" asked Dorothy. "Are you from there? Do they all talk funny, like you?"

"I do not talk funny!" protested Alice.

27

"Oh, I didn't mean..." Dorothy patted the girl's arm. "I just meant, you sound like you're from somewhere else."

Alice laughed. "*You* sound funny," she said. "They talk like me in Odds."

Dorothy frowned. "Then it *can't* be Oz," she sighed. "I was hoping it could be the same place."

"There's no such place as Oz," said the cat's smile, appearing in front of them. Both eyes showed up next, and blinked. "Oz isn't real." He blinked again and disappeared.

"Go away!" shouted Alice. "Stupid cat!" For no reason at all that Dorothy could tell, the other girl burst into tears.

"What's the matter?" asked Dorothy.

"Nothing," said Alice, still crying. She turned and started walking quickly back down the road.

"Are you all right?" said Dorothy.

"Leave me alone!" yelled the other girl, over her shoulder. Dorothy stopped and watched her as she went down the road.

"Poor girl," said Dorothy to Toto. Toto barked at Dorothy, then ran down the road after Alice. "Toto," yelled Dorothy, but the dog paid no heed. "Fine," said Dorothy, and followed.

Eventually they had gone some way down the road, though Dorothy didn't get too close to the girl, who seemed upset. But after some time, Alice turned and acknowledged Dorothy again. "Come on," she said, "I'll take you to Odds."

"Okay," said Dorothy.

After a little while, Alice said, "I suppose *you* aren't real, either."

"What?" said Dorothy, who was beginning to think Alice might be strange.

"That's what the cat says," said Alice, "that if you can go all the way down this road, you aren't real."

"I am too real," said Dorothy.

"Maybe," said Alice, shrugging. "I'm just telling you what the cat said. Real people are like your friends that tried to cross the stream. They shrink."

"You were spying on us!" said Dorothy.

"I wasn't spying," said Alice. "It was the cat. He told me to watch."

"I am real," said Dorothy.

"So am I," said Alice. "Or maybe I'm not." She seemed about to cry again. "Have you ever heard of Odds?" she asked.

"No," said Dorothy, "I don't think I ever have."

"I don't think Odds is real, either." She said, "I've never heard of Oz."

"Oz is real," said Dorothy. "I have friends there. Maybe it's past Odds."

"It could be," said Alice.

They came to a clearing and Toto, after doing dog business by one large rock, crossed to another rock on the other side and lay down.

"Come on, Toto," said Dorothy, but Toto ignored her and looked off to the side, then rested his chin down between his front paws.

"I don't think he's going anywhere," laughed Alice. "He wants to rest." She, too, sat down beside a rock, so Dorothy joined them, kicking off her slippers and wagging her toes.

"Yes, my feet could use the rest," said Dorothy. She noticed a smile growing behind Alice's head. "He does follow you," she said, pointing. Alice turned and grimaced. Toto growled.

"I wish your dog would bite him," said Alice.

Toto barked once. "That means Toto agrees with you," said Dorothy.

"Is Toto real?" Alice demanded of the cat's smirk.

"None of this is real," said the cat. And now they could see his eyes twinkling, and then a whisker. "It's all a dream."

"Whose dream?" demanded Alice.

"*Your* dream?" Dorothy added.

"Someone's dream," said the cat, grinning. "Someone's always dreaming. It makes one curious."

"I'm *most* curious," said Alice to the cat, "as to who invited *you*."

The cat winked. "Everyone's invited," he said, "to the Dreamer's Ball." And then, all at once, he appeared fully, his claws grasping a tree branch like a wingless bat's, his skinny body hanging upside down. He let go of the branch with his front paws, stretching toward the little girls like a kitten reaching for a ball of yarn, then let go with the other paws and fell, disappearing into the air before he hit the ground.

"What a strange cat," said Dorothy.

"I hate him," Alice said.

"But," said Dorothy, "you do have to admit, it all feels very like a dream."

"Perhaps this is what *your* dreams are like," said Alice. "Mine are rather more pleasant."

She certainly can be disagreeable, thought Dorothy. "In any case," said Dorothy, "I certainly feel real enough to me." At that, Toto barked and stood up, shaking himself vigorously before continuing down the road.

"I suppose it's time to move on, then," said Alice. She stood up and offered a hand to Dorothy, helping her to her feet. They both followed Toto down the road to Odds.

But when they had gone a little more distance, to their surprise, the road came to an abrupt end in a patch of grass beside a small cottage made of brick that shone red in the afternoon sun, a tiny chimney on the roof bubbling small clouds of white smoke. "I thought you said this road went to Odds," said Dorothy.

"I thought it did," said Alice, her face wrinkled in consternation. "I guess it must be the other direction."

"Well, we've come a long way," said Dorothy, "for you not to know for sure."

"I thought it was this direction," said Alice. "It has to be. I've never gone past the stream going the other way." She looked over at the cottage. "Maybe we took a wrong turn."

We haven't turned at all, thought Dorothy. But all she said was, "Maybe."

"We could ask for directions here," said Alice, still looking at the house. Dorothy didn't say anything, so after a moment Alice walked up the short path to the door of the cottage and rapped loudly.

"What if it's a witch?" said Dorothy, quietly, but Alice just shrugged. After a moment, the door opened, revealing a young, beautiful woman with a rather stern expression that softened when she saw the two girls.

31

"Can I help you?" she said.

"Yes, thank you, please, ma'am," said Alice politely, "we were looking for the road to Odds, and seem to have lost our way."

"The road to Oz, you say?" said the woman, and Alice shook her head, but at the same time Dorothy's face lit up.

"You know how to get to Oz?" she said. "No one seems to have heard of it."

"Of course I know Oz," said the woman, pointing. "It's that way, straight down the road."

"But that's where we've come from," said Dorothy.

"It's pretty far," said the woman. "You must have headed the wrong direction."

"But you've never heard of Odds?" said Alice.

"Odds?" repeated the woman, articulating carefully. "No, never," she said, "but it's probably that way, too. Not much happening the other way." She hooked a thumb over her shoulder, indicating past her cottage.

"Well, thank you for your help," said Dorothy, "but if Oz is as far as you say, we need to be getting a move on."

"You girls are making the trip alone?" asked the woman.

"We have Toto," Dorothy explained.

"I see," said the woman. "Then be safe. But if you come this way again—"

"I doubt we will," interrupted Dorothy. "It's awfully far."

"Well, if you do," the woman said, "my name's Pandora, and you're welcome to stop here if you need."

"Thank you," said Alice. "You've been very kind."

They left the house and started back down the road,

going back where they had come, until they came to the same clearing with the stones, and once again Toto sat to rest and the girls joined him. "Are you going to go to Oz with us?" Dorothy asked Alice.

"Might as well," said Alice. "I don't have anywhere else to go." And behind them they heard a snicker and saw a disappearing cat. Toto barked and continued down the road, and the girls followed.

"I have lots of friends in Oz," said Dorothy. "I think you will like them." She had no idea if that was true (or if her friends would like Alice, either), but she thought it was the nice thing to say.

"I'm sure I will," said Alice, who also didn't know if that was true.

Shortly, though, to their surprise, they came again upon the same cottage at the end of the road.

"What?" said Dorothy. "Did we go the wrong direction again?"

"I don't see how," said Alice.

"It's Toto's fault," said Dorothy. "I guess we just weren't thinking when we followed the dog."

"I guess," said Alice, doubtfully. "Should we knock and say hello?"

"Let's just get going to Oz," said Dorothy. "Look how much time we've lost already."

So they turned around again and went down the road, but it wasn't long before once again they were facing the cottage where the lane narrowed to an end.

"I don't understand," said Dorothy. "How did we get turned around again?"

Alice ignored her and knocked on the cottage door.

"Hello, Miss Pandora," she said when the door opened. "We seem to have gotten lost again."

"Oh, dear," said Pandora. "I was afraid you'd come back."

"What do you mean?" said Alice.

"Somehow we got turned around," said Dorothy.

"Yes," said Pandora, "that's what I was afraid of."

"I don't understand," said Alice, and behind them a cat appeared and giggled.

"Oh, hush," said Pandora, to the cat. "Poor girls," she said, to Alice and Dorothy, "you've wandered too far."

"There's no going back now," said the cat, in a jolly manner, and Alice burst into tears.

"I can't go home?" she asked. "I've been looking for such a long time."

"I thought you were looking for Odds," said Dorothy, surprised. "Is Odds home?"

"She's been lost a long time, I think," said Pandora. "Poor thing," she said to Alice, putting her arms around her gently. "Were you ever real at all?"

Alice broke angrily out of her embrace. "I *am* real," she said. "Come on, Dorothy, let's get out of here." She marched down the road, away from the house.

"Am I real?" Dorothy asked the woman, but Pandora, her eyes soft and sympathetic, took a moment before shaking her head no. "Come on, Toto," said Dorothy, and they followed Alice away.

But barely had the cottage disappeared in the distance behind them when it appeared in the distance before them, once again. Pandora stood waiting at the open door for them.

"She is a witch," said Alice. "We should have known."

"I'm no witch," said Pandora. "I just live in this strange place."

"You can't get out, either," said Dorothy. "Is that it? You're stuck here?"

"You can live with me here, if you'd like," Pandora said. "There are no others here yet, but they will come."

"And be stuck here?" protested Dorothy. "There's no way out, is there?"

"To become real?" said Pandora. "That's what you're asking, isn't it?"

"Yes," said Dorothy, after a pause.

"You've never been real," said Pandora. "What you're missing is an illusion."

"I am real," Alice said.

Dorothy thought of Aunt Em, and Kansas.

"But there is a way," said Pandora, "for dreams to take life. I have a way right here in my home." She opened the door a little wider. "You *can* become real."

"I can leave here? I can go home?" said Dorothy. "Or to Oz?"

"If your home is real, you can go there."

"I *know* Kansas is real," said Dorothy. "And I'm pretty sure about Oz."

"Then I have a passage," said Pandora, "a gate you can use. Come with me." And she went into the cottage, leaving the door ajar. After a moment, Dorothy followed, and behind her came Toto, then Alice, her face set in a grimace.

She led them through another door, to a back room, where a large decorated jar stood in the center. It was made of an opaque, almost mirror-like glass, shaped almost like a raindrop, with the bottom wider than the top, and it was huge – easily large enough to hold a man.

"Look inside," Pandora told Dorothy, indicating a step-ladder next to the jar. Dorothy climbed five steps, enough to get her head over the top to where she could look down into it.

"It's black," she said. "I don't see the bottom."

"There isn't one," said Pandora.

"It comes out in China on the other side?" asked Dorothy.

"No," said Pandora, "it's just a short trip to reality."

"You want to see?" said Dorothy to Toto, who was making snarfing noises at the base of the ladder. Dorothy picked him up and brought him to the top, letting him look down into the darkness. He craned his neck to look in, then looked back at Dorothy, grinning. "Well," said Dorothy, "I trust you, Toto."

And with that, Toto jumped out of her arms and into the jar, disappearing into the darkness.

"Toto!" Dorothy yelled after him.

"He's fine," said Pandora. "Go, you can meet him on the other side."

"Ah, reality," said the cat, licking his only visible paw. "A consummation devoutly to be wished."

"Alice, are you coming, too?" Dorothy asked, already climbing into the jar. "I know you'll like Oz."

"I'm already real," said Alice, sternly. "Ask her why she doesn't go through the jar, if it is what she says it is."

Dorothy hesitated, one leg still holding her weight on the ladder. "Why don't you, Pandora?"

"I like it here," said Pandora. "I like to dream." She looked at Alice. "But then, I was never real to begin with."

"I have to find Toto," said Dorothy. "Come on, Alice." She climbed in and disappeared over the edge of Pandora's jar.

"So how about it?" asked Pandora. "Are you going with her? Or are you going to stay here with me?" She seemed patient, and kind, even to Alice, who still didn't trust her. "It's all right to be a dream," she said, "but it's good to be real, too, if that's what you want."

"I am real," said Alice. "I can go where I want." And she walked out of the cottage and down the road. But eventually it appeared before her again. The cat sat on the doorstep, the door closed behind it.

"She knew you would strike again," the cat giggled, "like lightning."

"Disappear for me," said Alice. "I like it when you do that."

The cat faded away to a bare mocking grin.

It's a curious world, thought Alice. She watched the closed door in front of her and started walking backward, thinking, I know it's behind me now, eventually I will bump into Pandora's closed door and it will open when she thinks I'm knocking. I will watch myself bump into it, she thought, if I can see far enough. Won't that be a funny sight.

And she kept walking backward until the cottage disappeared from her view, though she strained to see it. And she thought, any second, I will trip over the porch step and fall and hurt my head. The cat will laugh at me.

But now she saw she was passing the clearing with the

stones, and though she wanted to turn around and see if she had gotten away, she didn't. I'll just keep walking backwards, she thought, until I get home.

And after some time her feet stepped into the water of a stream, and after she had crossed it, she heard a voice, scolding, saying, "Alice! Where have you been? And look what you've done to your dress!"

"I'm sorry," said Alice, turning around and facing her sister. "I got lost, chasing a cat into the forest."

"Daydreaming," said her sister, "always daydreaming. When will you ever wake up?"

Books

Kristen said, "You have to get rid of some of these.
They're piling up again."

Since she was standing next to a bookshelf,
Ronnie thought she must mean his books. He had to
admit, they were starting to get out of hand. He had
started to pile books on top of the bookcases; he had
already run out of room behind and on top of the shelved
books. Some were even running over onto the
entertainment center and the pool table.

He sighed. "Let me finish this," he said, referring to his
crossword puzzle. "I'm ranked fourth," he said, "I think I'm
doing good on this one."

"That's wonderful," said Kristen. "Just don't forget to go
through the books."

"I won't," he said, and he didn't. He filled in the final
word (metabolism: "animal fuel efficiency"), and walked
over to the biggest bookcase, the one that had drawn
Kristen's attention.

As always, he started by putting aside his favorites:
William Shakespeare, Edgar Poe, Stephen King. These
were the ones that caused him physical pain when he
contemplated throwing them out. He didn't have to get rid

of everything; Kristen would not ask that. But just enough so that they weren't spilling over so badly, so that he could organize them a bit more neatly.

Kristen, he knew, would want him to arrange them all by height and relative thickness, or some such thing. Screw that, he thought, shoving them into the shelves. His only requirement in shelving was that you could see the title and the author.

Once, Kristen had removed all the dust jackets and tried to arrange them by the color of the binding. Ronnie, who recognized book covers better than faces, had noticed as soon as he walked in the door. He had been furious.

"Are you crazy?" he had asked. "Don't take the dust jackets off. Those are there to protect the books."

"But look how nice they look," she had protested.

He didn't think they looked nice. He thought they looked ridiculous, like an art project instead of a book collection. (Truthfully, he had experienced a strange guilty thrill seeing all the books so exposed like that, the colors choreographed like a literary kick line.) He had collected the dust jackets, minus a few that had been ruined, from the garbage can in the kitchen.

"I almost shredded them," she said, without apology.

"Don't do that again," he had said, angry at the time.

He smiled as he thought of it now, knowing he had probably overreacted. But she had respected the collection since then, leaving its distribution in his hands, merely remarking those times they started to spill over into the living space.

He sighed, and continued working through the books in the cases. Some of them he could bear to get rid of.

Fifteen books or so. Maybe twelve. Just enough to get them all back onto the shelves again.

*****

The first thing Kristen noticed when she walked in from work was the mess of books, and she couldn't help feeling a stab of irritation. She had thought Ronnie had been going through them to remove some; instead, it looked like, if anything, there were even more of them here.

He had all day to take care of this, she thought. She didn't exactly resent his summers off – Ronnie was a teacher at the high school – but still, sometimes it irritated her to have to come home from a hard day at work to see he had been sitting all day doing nothing.

Especially when she had specifically asked him to do something. Not like it was a huge chore, either. Just get rid of a few of these books, that's all. Straighten up just a tad.

She found Ronnie sprawled on the bed, doing a crossword. That's what he's been doing all day, she thought. That's *all* he's been doing.

"I thought I asked you to take care of some of the books," she said. Ronnie looked up, a startled look on his face.

"My love," he said, "I didn't hear you come in." He closed the crossword book and came to kiss her on the cheek. "How was work?" he asked.

"Fine," she said. "I thought you were going to straighten the books."

He looked momentarily confused. "I did," he said. "I got them all back on the shelves." Kristen frowned. "I took ten

41

or twelve of them down to Library Friends," Ronnie said.

"And how many did you buy while you were there?" Kristen said, an edge to her voice.

"I didn't," protested Ronnie. "I didn't buy anything."

"Ronald," Kristen said.

"Don't talk to me like I'm a child," Ronnie said.

"I'm sorry," said Kristen, but she didn't sound it. "Just, could you straighten the books tomorrow, please?"

"Okay," said Ronnie. "Fine, not a problem."

*****

She is trying to play a trick on me, he thought, when he saw the books. She bought a lot of books and stacked them around and is pretending that I'm not cleaning up my mess. Trying to be funny, maybe.

She hadn't seemed like she was trying to be funny.

Doesn't make much sense, though, he thought. To go buy a bunch of books and then tell me to get rid of them.

He picked up a book at random, one he didn't recognize. *Jesus and Furniture-Making*, by Harold Lawrence. He shrugged, thinking, never heard of it. Another was *Hocus Semetary*, by Kurt King.

She must have bought a bunch at random, Ronnie thought, shaking his head. Strange joke. I'll box up the new ones and get them out of the way.

He gathered all the new books, the ones he didn't recognize, and put them in the back of the closet. I'll see what she wants to do with those later, he thought. Crazy female.

*****

When Kristen saw the books the next morning, on her

42

way out the door to work, she thought to herself, He is doing this deliberately. He's trying to annoy me.

I will not let it bother me, she thought, as she squealed out of the driveway.

*****

When Ronnie saw the books, he thought, She's gone crazy. What am I supposed to do with all these? Whatever she was doing, it had gone well beyond what might be considered funny.

That's got to be fifty or more books she's added, he thought, looking around the room.

He counted forty-seven by the time he was done. He hadn't heard of any of them. Don't know where she's getting these, he thought. Woman doesn't know a good book from a bean bag.

There were eleven more stacked on the box he had put away the night before. He found them when he was going to take them all to the Library Friends, and stood looking at them, shaking his head.

She really has gone crazy, he thought.

He put the two boxes in the trunk and drove to the library. "More?" asked Carly, the girl who worked the Library Friends desk.

"Yeah," said Ronnie, "stuff I don't want."

Carly looked at one of the covers. "*Tale of Two Vampires*?" she said. "Not your usual, Mr. Grosz."

"It's something Kristen got," said Ronnie. "I've never heard of it. Or the author either."

"'Charles Rice,'" she read. "Name sounds familiar." She shrugged. "Where's your wife getting these books, Mr.

43

Grosz? The ones you brought in yesterday, I couldn't find any of them in the database."

"I don't know," Ronnie said, "I haven't asked her. What's wrong with them?" He was worried she was going to make him take them back.

"Oh, nothing's wrong with them. Just, you know, I couldn't find any of the ISBN numbers, in the LOC database. You know, to stack them."

"Is that a problem?"

"Oh, no, no problem, Mr. Grosz. I just made some new entries." She shrugged, chewing gum noisily. "The library appreciates the donations. You're a true Library Friend."

I think she's making fun of me, Ronnie thought. "Thanks," he said. But it is generous, he thought in the car on the way back, to be giving them so many books.

*****

There was one book, apparently he had missed, sitting on the table in the kitchen. *Crossword Clues* it said, published by PuzzleFest.

She set this one aside separate, Ronnie thought. She knew I'd like this one. It wouldn't be complete (no *way* it could be complete!), but PuzzleFest published the contest he was working on.

Some of the answers will be in there, he thought. Maybe even one or two I can't figure out.

Well, unlikely. He wondered where she got the book. They wouldn't let the really difficult ones out, of course. They wouldn't want the contest to be too easy.

I'm going to win it this year. Maybe the book could help. I'll have to thank her when she gets home, he thought.

*****

"You're trying to piss me off," said Kristen, looking at the pile of books.

She's really lost it, thought Ronnie, also looking at the pile of books. She's gone off the deep end. "Honey?" he said. "Are you okay?"

"Whoa, Nellie," Kristen said.

She's talking nonsense, thought Ronnie. He could tell she was about to boil over, too. She had that pinched white look around the nose. "Are you mad?" he said, the most dangerous question, but he couldn't stop himself from asking.

"You want me to be mad?" Almost lost control of your voice a little there at the end, she thought. Felt it squeaking. Lose the fury, she thought. He wants you to be mad.

"I'll donate the books," he said. He thought maybe she was dangerous.

"Please do," she said tightly.

*****

He tried. Day after day, he tried. She must be spending a fortune on these things, he thought, after about the third week. Eventually Carly at the library said he had to slow down. "I can't keep up with the database, Mr. Grosz."

"You don't want my books?" he said.

"Why don't you try selling some of them to the used shop, down on Berry," she suggested.

"Good idea," he said. He drove down there and saw where they were offering 15 cents a book. Ripoff, he

45

thought. But he had been donating them to the library anyway.

The man at the counter said, "I can give you 5 cents for these."

"What?" protested Ronnie. "Your sign says 15."

"I can't do that," said the clerk. "That's for listed books. These aren't on the list."

"It doesn't say anything about listed books on the sign," said Ronnie.

"Hey, that's our policy," said the little man with the goatee.

It's more than I was asking from the Library Friends, thought Ronnie. "Fine," he said, "I'll take it."

*****

He still brought a few books by the library every now and then. "Money isn't everything," he told Carly. "I'm still a Friend." Making fun of himself, a little bit.

He's flirting with me, Carly thought. She didn't mind. He wasn't bad looking. He had lost some of that skinniness he used to have, he was starting to fill out in the chest a bit.

At home, Ronnie had the shelves once again in order before Kristen came home from work. He knew he would have to come out in the middle of the night, again. Possibly even once more before the morning. Her insanity seemed to know no end. I don't know how she does it, he thought. Always more books, always sneaking around, always lying. No wonder she looks so tired all the time, he thought.

For him it boiled over that night. He didn't see it

coming; he just said, out of the blue, "I'm tired of it."

"You're tired of what?" she said. It was more of a snarl, as though she'd been waiting all along for it. A challenge.

"The books," he said. "The books have got to stop."

"Ronnie," she said, "I'm leaving."

"You don't have to leave," he said. "Just, I can't keep up with the books."

"I'm leaving, Ronnie," she said again. And she left.

*****

He spent some time being depressed about it. Still, he knew it was just the craziness, whatever psychosis she'd developed. She continued, even separated, somehow to pile the house with books. She must spy on me, he thought. I know she loves me.

He didn't worry so much about cleaning them all up, or donating them. Really, he thought it unique, this expression of her love for him. She knows I love books, he thought. With the money he won from the crossword contest, he sent money to her new address. He hardly saw her, but he left the door unlocked for her, so she could act out her mixed-up fantasy.

It creeped Carly out a little, thinking about the crazy wife. Still, it was like Ronnie said. She didn't seem dangerous. And some of the books she brought had turned out to be pretty good.

She had high hopes for the one she was about to read. Carly shrugged on one of Ronnie's bigger shirts and stretched out on his bed. She picked up the book: *Crime & Electric Sheep*. About an android who commits murder and has strange dreams about the consequences. She had never heard of the author – Fyodor Dick – but it sounded fascinating.

Above All Earthly Dignities

by Kyle Staples

D anny was sitting on the toilet in the stall of the boy's bathroom, minding his own business. He was going to be late for class, there wasn't any doubt about that, but when you had to go, you had to go, and Danny thought he would be going for a while. He might even skip class, he hadn't decided yet. But he hadn't finished his homework last night, and sometimes it was better not to show up in Miss Akton's at all rather than show up without your homework.

He should have brought a book. He did that sometimes, brought something to read into the stall with him. Nobody ever noticed, which was a good thing, since he was sure it was something you got made fun of for. He didn't get made fun of much anymore, mostly because people had stopped noticing him. And that was fine.

The graffiti on the door of the stall said, "Deck the stalls with these big balls." Not Stephen King, but not bad, considering. Underneath that it said, "DEEZ NUTZ!" And under that, "Rayland was fucking here," which had been crossed out and replaced with "Rayland was here, fucking" and a stick picture of people having sex. Danny knew Rayland, and he didn't have any trouble at all believing Rayland might have been fucking here. Most of the girls Danny knew would have loved to fuck Rayland, if they hadn't already. As for Danny, and just about every guy in Danny's crowd, he just tried to stay out of Rayland's way.

Then, right on cue, the bathroom door opened, and Danny heard Rayland's voice.

"In here."

And then a girl's voice, one he didn't recognize, "Ray, that's the boy's."

"So?"

"So I can't go in the boy's."

"Yeah, who's gonna tell? There ain't nobody in there."

Danny lifted his feet off the ground and prayed to God Rayland didn't come looking in his stall.

"I just don't like it. I've never been in the boy's before."

"Look, will you just fuckin' come on? You want to get caught?"

She must have decided to come in, then, because the bathroom door closed and the conversation continued. "Yuck, this place is dirty." She walked to the sinks, to where Danny could look down and see her tennis shoes, lined in pink, and red socks rolled down to her ankles. "How do you guys stand it?"

"What's wrong with it?"

"It's dirty."

"I like it. I hang out in here all the time." He walked over to stand behind her, and now Danny could see his tennis shoes, too. Danny tried to hold his breath. Rayland

50

took a step forward, until his Nikes were right behind her Nikes, almost touching.

When she spoke again, she sounded a little nervous. "Hey, Ray, give me a little space." The sink came on, quietly.

"I've been giving you space. I'm tired of space."

"Well, I still want space." Then, after a short silence, "Dammit, Ray, I'm trying to do my makeup."

So Rayland stepped back and his feet disappeared from view. Danny started breathing again, slowly and carefully. The bathroom was getting hot. He couldn't think anything other than, *Please, please, please, please don't look in this stall.* Over and over again.

Rayland said, "What do you think you need all that shit for? You look okay without it."

"Gee, thanks."

"Okay, you look good without it. That what you want me to say? You look like a model. Or an actress."

"That's better."

"You know what, though, what the difference between you and an actress is?"

"What?"

"They put out."

"You know what, Ray? You're a shit head."

"Hell, they put out right there on the screen. In front of everybody."

"So?"

"So what I'm saying, maybe they look better, just because they put out." He came back to the sinks, right next to the stalls. His shoes were right there. The metal creaked, Danny knew Rayland was leaning against it. He

51

thought, *Please please please please.*

Rayland said, "Why don't you?"

"What, put out?"

Rayland said, "Shit, you won't even give a guy a little head. Every girl in this whole school, every one, wants it from me."

"Please."

"Yeah, that's what they say. 'Please! Oh, please, Ray! Put it in me!'"

The girl said, "Whatever," and, surprising and frightening Danny, Ray exploded. His feet moved up to the girl's, and the metal of the stall shook when he hit it. Danny shut his eyes, scared.

Ray's voice was low, tight, when he said, "Whatever me, bitch." There was a small, frightened sound from the girl, a little gasp, and then the whole stall shook. Danny opened his eyes. He could see by the girl's feet, Rayland was holding her against the stall. It was quiet then, for just a few seconds, with nothing but the heavy sound of Ray's and the girl's breathing. And Danny's own beneath it, stifled. Danny closed his eyes again, he couldn't keep them open.

Then there was a rustling sound, fabric on fabric. The girl made another sound, started to say something. It was slapped short, the girl gasping, and Rayland, whispering, "Shut up. Just be quiet. You scream, I'll break your fucking neck."

Some more rustling of clothing. Danny could hear, just barely, the girl crying. He knew what was going on. He thought to himself, *You should do something.* But the thought was cut short, as the stall started shaking, in a slow but quickening rhythm. His head was beating with it. Saying, *Please, please, please...*

*****

After they were gone, he just waited in the silence. For a long time.

Rayland had gone first, as soon as he was done. He had simply said, "You ever say something about this... Don't ever." And left the girl crying. She had burst into louder sobs when the door shut behind him, sobs that seemed to go on forever. Danny listened to her, feeling horrible, his chest burning and his throat blocked, knowing there was nothing he could do. Until finally she stopped, ran the sink for a bit, and left.

And he sat there. Guilt shivered through him, guilt at his own feebleness, but more than that was the relief, the simple pleasure of being able to breathe fully, to let his lips get moisture and his belly puff out.

Eventually he cleaned up, opened the stall, and stepped around. And was startled, scared out of his wits, because, sitting calmly on the sink was a boy, maybe three or four years younger than his own thirteen years.

He and the boy looked at each other silently, Danny wondering how he hadn't heard the boy come in. The boy had a little frown on his face. He was watching Danny's eyes, and Danny felt the guilt tingle all over him again. The boy said, quietly, "You heard that?"

Danny said, "Who are you?"

The little boy shook his head. He said, "Why didn't you do anything?"

Danny went to the sink next to him, turned it on,

53

washed his hands. He said, "I don't know what you're talking about."

"You heard it."

Danny was mad, he was scared. He could feel his eyes starting to burn. He said, "Shut up. I don't know you. I don't know what you're talking about?" He wouldn't cry.

He turned away from the boy, wanting to leave, wanting to get away from the boy, but he could hear him behind him. Jumping down from the sink, following him. Saying, "Why didn't you do anything?"

And he turned back, not wanting to say anything, but having to. Almost shouting, "What about you? Why didn't you do anything?" The boy just shook his head again. Danny pushed him in the chest. "Who are you? You aren't old enough to be here! Go away!" He wanted to know what was going on. Had the boy seen everything? Why hadn't Rayland seen him? But the boy obviously wasn't answering any questions. Just shaking his head, back and forth.

Danny pushed the bathroom door open, running away. Running down the hall, down the stairs, around the corner, around another corner. Looking behind him. When he saw the boy wasn't following, he slowed. Walking. Finally crying.

*****

He went to Miss Akton's class after all, but only for ten minutes, since he was forty minutes late. She didn't say anything about it, though, or about his missing homework. Just gave him a look when he came in, and went right on with the class.

He had time to calm himself in that ten minutes, to breathe deeply, to say to himself, *See, it's all over, it's just over.* But he was the first one out when the bell rang, and he rushed to his next class. He didn't want to stop, didn't want to see or talk to anybody. He found himself, though, glancing around for Rayland. And looking down at tennis shoes, thinking, *Is that her? Is that her?*

He was scared again, five minutes into the next class, when he glanced behind him and there, sitting three rows back, was the boy. Just sitting there, looking at him. A boy Danny was sure had never been in this class before. Still with that little frown, that questioning look in the eyes. Danny could still hear him asking, "Why didn't you do anything?"

He wanted to say, wanted to scream, *What could I do? Hey, what could I do?*

He kept turning around. Kept glancing back at the boy. The girl behind him was giving him questioning looks he tried to ignore. Halfway through class, he saw it clearly, the boy silently mouthed, "What are you going to do?"

He thought about that. Realizing he probably could do something. He was scared, though, scared of Rayland. Scared of the girl in the bathroom.

Eventually, though, he raised his hand. It was quivering and only half in the air, but Mr. Simmons saw it. Danny said, nervous, "Mr. Simmons, I need to go see the principal."

Mr. Simmons said, "What about?"

Danny looked at all the faces in the room, looking at him. He said, through a tense throat, "I think... I don't think I should say."

Mr. Simmons looked at him funny but let him go. The door was in the back of the room, but he went all the way around the front of his row, rather than walk by the boy. He could feel the boy's eyes on him, out the door, and even down the hall, even though he knew there was no one behind him.

Mr. Knight, the principal, was out in the secretary's office, and Danny ignored the secretary's "Can I help you," instead looking pleadingly at Mr. Knight. Mr. Knight looked over at him and Danny tried to say something. He couldn't at first, but then, at the growing look of concern on Mr. Knight's face, he got out, "Rayland." Then, finally, "Rayland Burnick."

Mr. Knight said to the secretary, "Linda, we'll discuss it later, okay?" He took Danny into his office, sat him in a chair in front of his desk, then took another, next to him. He said, "What about Rayland, did he hurt you?"

Danny shook his head. "No, it wasn't me... A girl."

Mr. Knight said, "Hey, it's okay, tell me what happened."

Danny did, all he could. He left out everything about the boy on the sink, because it just confused and scared him, and he wasn't sure it was relevant. But he told about hearing Rayland, about seeing the girl's shoes, about hearing them against the stall, and knowing, with his eyes shut, what was going on.

Mr. Knight had questions. He answered them. Mr. Knight sat back in his chair. He was rubbing his index finger and his thumb together, thinking, and finally he said, "You aren't making this up?" Not accusing, just questioning, and Danny said, "No, sir, not at all."

Mr. Knight said, "You don't know the girl. You're sure?"

Danny said, "No, sir. But wouldn't she have been late for second period?"

Mr. Knight said, "If I have you sit out there, and I bring a girl in, or two, or three, would you be able to tell me if it was her?"

"I don't... I don't know, Mr. Knight, I don't... All I saw was her shoes. And I heard her voice. I don't know."

"But would you try?"

Danny swallowed, almost shook his head, but said, very quietly, "Yes, sir."

Mr. Knight said, "Okay. Danny, I'm going to have you sit out there in a chair by the door, okay, just sit there. And I'll bring somebody in, take her into my office, and if you think it's her, you tell Linda, okay? You don't even have to say anything, just nod or shake your head. And she'll give me a call in the office, okay? And you just wait, that's all."

"What if I don't know," Danny said, "or what if, I don't think it's her, I mean, if you bring them in and I don't think any of them are her."

Mr. Knight said, "Just do your best, okay?" and Danny nodded. They went out. Danny sat in the chair by the door, trying not to be scared. Mr. Knight went over to Linda, talked to her quietly for a few moments. She was nodding. Mr. Knight came over to him, said, "Okay, I know you're nervous. Just wait. This might take some time, don't worry about anything. I'm going to go into my office. If you feel like you need me, just come on in, okay?" Danny nodded. Mr. Knight went into his office. Linda gave him a reassuring smile. He tried to return it, but his face was stiff, and he gave it up.

It was maybe fifteen minutes later when the first girl came in. She looked at Danny, sitting there. He looked at her feet, she was wearing sandals. It definitely wasn't her, and he felt oddly relieved. She went up to Linda and said, "I'm supposed to see the principal." Linda waved her into Mr. Knight's office and gave him a questioning look. He shook his head. Linda picked up her phone, pushed a button, said, "No, not her," and hung up. A few minutes later, the girl came out, gave Danny another look, and walked out.

The second girl, though, ten minutes later, he found he didn't even have to look at her shoes or hear her voice. It was her, he knew it deep in his gut. His stomach clamped up, his breathing was shallow. He looked at her shoes, to be sure, and recognized them immediately. The pink lining, the red socks. He was almost scared to look at her face. But she was stopped in the doorway, looking at him, and he had to. Her face was tense. She was glaring at him, almost like she recognized him. He looked away, trying not to shiver.

She went up to the desk, said to Linda, "Mr. Knight wants to see me?" and Linda told her to go right in. Danny was already nodding, before the door closed behind her. Linda raised her eyebrows, Danny said, "I'm sure. I'm sure." Linda picked up her phone, pushed the button. She said, "That's her... Yes... Yes," and hung up.

Danny didn't know why he was so scared, but he could see in Linda's eyes how obvious it was. He looked down at his feet, waiting.

It took forever, it seemed, before the girl came out. She

was glaring hard at Danny now, staring him down as she went by. She stopped by the door again, looking down at him, then her eyes went up to where Mr. Knight and the secretary were watching her. She frowned, grimaced, then was gone.

He was shaking. He couldn't help it. Mr. Knight said, "Okay, Danny, you want to come on back in here?"

He got up. His legs were weak. He walked back into Mr. Knight's office, sat in the chair. Mr. Knight sat next to him. He said, after a moment's silence, "She said none of that happened. She said she didn't know what I was talking about."

Danny just looked at him. He didn't know what to say.

Mr. Knight said, "I think she was lying. I mean, it was obvious to me she was lying, and I believe you. Without a doubt. But I don't know that there's anything I can do about it." He scratched at his eyebrow. He said, "I will call her parents, I'll talk to them about it, I think that's all I can do. If she never admits it happened... I don't know what we can do."

Danny nodded, looking at the floor.

Mr. Knight said, "Danny, thank you. A lot of kids wouldn't have come in here." Danny didn't know what to say to that, either. Mr. Knight said, "Okay, I'm going to have Linda give you a pass back to class. If you want to talk about this again, just come on in, okay?"

*****

Danny was in the seventh grade. Rayland was in the eighth, so they didn't have lunch together. Danny was grateful for that, when he went to lunch after leaving the

59

office. He knew he would have to see Rayland again, eventually, but he didn't want to. Ever. Or the girl, whose name he didn't know.

But the little boy was there. No one else seemed to notice him, but Danny, sitting all by himself at the end of the table, couldn't avoid him when the boy sat down next to him.

The boy looked at him, watched him eating. The frown was gone, he just looked curious. He said, "Why'd you tell?"

Danny said, "Where's your lunch?" Because he didn't want to talk about it ever again.

But the boy shook his head, and said, "Why'd you tell?"

Danny said, frustrated, "Because you told me to. Why didn't you tell? Where were you?"

The boy said, "I was watching you."

Danny said, "Who are you? You don't go here."

The boy just shook his head again. Danny glared at him and ate his lunch. They were both silent until the bell rang.

*****

After school, Danny never made it to the bus. He was in the hall, pushing through the crowd. He could see the doors, propped open, the sunlight coming in. And then Rayland was in front of him, looking down at him, his eyes slitted and his jaw clenched. Rayland said, "Stay here." Danny tried to push past, anyway, but Rayland grabbed him by the shirt, lifting him up some, pushing him back.

Danny said, "Please," and Rayland moved in close and punched him in the stomach, hard, right in the middle of the crowd of students.

Rayland said, "You come with me, you fucker," and pushed him down the hall, away from the buses, against the flow of people. Danny didn't resist. He was retching a little, his stomach making little spastic motions.

Danny tried to say, "Somebody..." Rayland's forearm came hard into his back, his knees bent, and he almost fell.

Rayland pushed him down the hall, down to the other end, through the doors to the back of the building. There were a few kids there, some who walked, some waiting for their parents. Rayland dragged him away from these, down by the dumpsters, down by the alley and into it. Rayland threw him away from him.

Danny said, "Please," and Rayland punched him in the face. Danny saw it coming just barely, but didn't even have time to move. His face felt like it collapsed. His jaw went slack. His legs were softening. Rayland punched him again, in the same place, and Danny fell down onto his back, his mouth filling up with warm fluid.

Rayland said, "You little bitch," and kicked him in the stomach. Said, "Bastard," and kicked him in the face. Said, "Fucking prick," and came down to hit him, to punch him in the face and arms and neck. Rayland hit him and kicked him and slapped him. Danny was crying and not able to stop. He was whimpering. He was choking, gagging, trying to curl up, until his body was pulled open and kicked and punched some more.

Danny closed his eyes, watching the red grow and grow. He could hear Rayland cursing him, could feel the blows on his body, but they got farther and farther away as he watched the red grow.

*****

He couldn't open his eyes for a long time even after he knew Rayland was gone. They were crusted shut, it felt like, and Danny thought to himself, *Please, don't let that be blood.*

He rolled over onto his back, a motion that clenched his stomach, and he had to roll back to vomit. His eyes opened then, painfully. His vomit pooled red and thick.

He turned at the sound of footsteps behind him, and looked up, into the sun, into the shadow of the little boy. The boy was frowning again, that little frown between his eyebrows. He looked Danny over, and said, "Are you okay?"

Danny tried to stand up, but his legs wouldn't quite move under him. The boy held a hand out, and Danny took it. Together they pulled him to his feet. The boy took his hand away, looking at the blood that had gotten on his fingers. He said, "What are you going to do?"

Danny turned away from him. He limped back down the alley, towards the school. He stumbled. The boy said, behind him, "What are you going to do?"

Danny ignored him. He didn't look back until he got to the doors of the school. Then he took one quick glance. But the boy was gone.

To Dino-Dig Returneth

by Derek Cocker

There was once a boy named Ronnie who always had things come to life around him. I guess that might sound exciting, like something you might want, but really it wasn't. It caused him no end of trouble.

At one time, for instance, he had a dog named Chi-Chi. She was a tiny rectangular dog with barely any snout, and she used to bite all the children who tried to play with Ronnie. She was a mean dog, but she was Ronnie's best friend. He gave her a giant stuffed tiger he won at the fair. It was her favorite toy; she could bite and tear at it for hours. But when it came to life, Chi-Chi didn't have a chance – it was easily three times her size. They say the tiger ate her in one gulp.

Other things came to life, too. Once his homework got up and ran into the kitchen and jumped in the garbage disposal. He tried to explain this to his kindergarten teacher. "The garbage disposal ate my homework." The teacher didn't believe him, and I'm sure he would have been put in the corner if the stapler hadn't attacked at just that moment.

The first time I ever saw something come to life around Ronnie, we were sitting at the children's museum where I volunteered. I was helping him build castles out of blocks in the hands-on play area. Really, I was doing most of the building. Ronnie had a Pound Puppy under one arm and was sucking his thumb.

"Once," he said, "when my Mommy was going to work my Daddy came out naked."

I said, "What? He went outside naked?"

"No, not outside." Ronnie giggled, put his Pound Puppy on the counter and went around to sit on the other side of the block castle, facing me. He said, "He came out of his room, and he was naked and had on his underwear, and he tripped over my dog Chi-Chi, and he fell, and Chi-Chi bit him, and he said, 'Fudge.'" I put another block on the top of the castle. "I know," said Ronnie, "I'm not supposed to say, 'Fudge.'"

"That's right, you shouldn't," I said.

Ronnie said, "When my Daddy said, 'fudge,' and he was naked," –giggle– "my Mommy went right over from the door and spanked him on his butt."

"Ah," I said.

"I was seven years old then," said Ronnie.

"How old are you now?" I asked, trying to change the subject.

"Seven."

"Oh," I said.

Ronnie said, "I'm seven. My doggy is seven, but he's older than that in doggy years, guess how old."

I counted on my fingers. "Forty-nine."

Ronnie laughed, picking up the Pound Puppy and hitting me with it. "No, that would be *old*. He's twenty-four, my Mommy said so." He gnawed at the end of the stuffed animal's nose. "His name is Arf, he goes everywhere I go. I mean everywhere. He's my best friend, after Chi-Chi. Chi-Chi's my other dog, but she can't go everywhere with me because Mommy says dogs aren't allowed in museums." He shrugged, looking puzzled. "I don't know why Arf can go. He gets to go everywhere. Arf goes to bed with me, and he goes to the store with me, and he goes to the bathroom with me. But he doesn't go to the shower with me. He doesn't like to be clean."

I accidentally dropped one of the blocks, knocking a part of the castle down. "I'll fix it," said Ronnie.

"He doesn't like to be clean?" I said.

"No way! Not ever. I've had him since I was five. He's never been cleaned, ever, not once." He finished fixing that part of the castle, then sat down on another, knocking a large portion over. Suddenly he stood up, laying the puppy down on top of the castle. "Can I leave Arf here for a second?" he said urgently. "I have to go!" And he ran out.

I used a block to push Arf onto the floor so I could continue building.

When Ronnie came back, I said, "I thought you took Arf everywhere?"

Ronnie shook his head. Very seriously, he said, "No way, Arf doesn't like these potties."

"The restrooms?" I said. "At the museum?"

"He only likes the one at home," he said. "Once, he went in one with me and I put him on the floor and he got white icky stuff on him."

"Ew," I said. "You cleaned it off, right?"

He shook his head. "He doesn't like to be cleaned. It came off on the carpet." He turned Arf over in his hands, maybe looking for a stain. "Do you want to hold him?" he asked.

I shook my head, taking a close look at it. It looked mangy. That was when it came to life, looking back at me and barking. It jumped out of Ronnie's arms and ran onto my leg, its soft stuffed feet tickling through my jeans, and bit me on my arm. It didn't hurt, I hardly felt the cloth teeth at all. Still, I was startled, and screamed a little. The Pound Puppy barked furiously and ran off.

"Oh no," said Ronnie, looking at me like it was my fault. "Arf!" he yelled, chasing after it. "Come back, Arf!"

After that, I saw that kind of thing happen around Ronnie just about enough to think hardly anything of it. Usually it wasn't too bad. Once, a kid's stroller got a little independent and wheeled itself up three floors before we recovered the poor toddler it was carrying, and another time two of the cardboard swordfish in the Kindergarten Aquarium started fencing. Of course, we all got just a little on edge whenever he walked into the museum, since there was no telling what could happen.

I remember the *last* time I ever saw something come to life around Ronnie, too. I think most everyone remembers that day. I was volunteering at the children's museum as I do every Thursday. I was working on the fourth floor, in the dinosaur exhibit. We got the word immediately when Ronnie arrived. Paul, one of the guys from the reception area, came running up, panting.

"Everyone," he said, "Ronnie's here, so be on your

toes."

"Be ready for anything," I told the new girl, standing next to me.

But there was no getting ready for that day, no.

At first it seemed it would be one of the more uneventful Ronnie days. A half-hour passed in which I did nothing more than sift sand in the Dino-Dig with a toddler in pigtails. I had almost forgotten about Ronnie entirely, thinking maybe he wouldn't come to our floor at all.

That's when I heard the first screams.

They were muffled, and distant. Probably I wouldn't have heard anything at all had there not been so many of them.

"What's that?" asked the new girl, looking a bit unnerved.

"I don't know," I said, "It must be Ronnie." The screams were getting louder. "Don't worry, he's just this annoying little boy," I said. But I have to admit I wasn't feeling too sure of myself.

Then someone came running in from Rusty's Railroad, yelling, "Bugs! Bugs!" and someone came in from the Mummy exhibit yelling "Spiders! Spiders!" and I remembered the new invertebrate display downstairs. It had been quite a splash, really, with hundreds of model insects and arachnids and such things hanging by string from the ceilings and stuck to walls. Made by kids from one of the local high schools, they had looked amazingly life-like, I had thought.

They looked even more life-like as they came flying through the door marked "Gravity Well" which some panicking fool had gotten his leg caught in, leaving it open.

"Oh, my God!" yelled the new girl, and I saw a plastic locust land on her hair and start pulling at the roots with its forelegs. It was trailing a long string of fishing-line tied to a little hook in its back. "Get it off me!" she screamed.

I slapped at it, but by the time I got it off she had a paper mache bumblebee the size of a grapefruit crawling on her back so I took a quick swipe at that and decided to run instead.

I dashed into the Koala Maze, not seeing any of the insects coming from that direction, and knowing it came out on the other side near the stairs. Some of the insects tried to follow me, but I squashed a cardboard cockroach and swatted a butterfly made out of construction paper and was able to make it into the stairwell.

It was a wasted effort. I met a crowd of people running up the stairs, looking stricken. Some pushed past me, and before I knew it I was stuck in the mob, being shoved back up to the fourth floor.

"What's going on?" I asked, trying to be heard over children screaming and women crying.

"The carousel," said one man, his voice cracking. "The carousel! The unicorn ran off with my boy!"

By this time we had been forced back into the Koala Maze, where the crowd thinned a bit as people took the various passages and got trapped. We could hear them shouting through the thin walls, "I'm stuck," or, "I'm lost," and some of the men had already started trying to pound through the plywood walls to get to the exit.

I ran back to the maze entrance. Most of the insects had apparently moved on, though tattered remains such as pipe-cleaner antennae and wire mandibles littered the floor.

I heard a wave of screams from Rusty's Railroad, so I went the other way, towards the Pyramid with the Mummy behind the glass. If I made it through that I would come out by the main ramps, which twisted down to the front entrance.

I had just stepped through the door when I heard someone yelling behind me, "Wait, wait!" I turned and saw Ronnie, just coming from Rusty's Railroad, stepping out into the Dino-Dig. He tripped over a plastic shovel and started crying.

"Ronnie," I said, "quit crying. Get a hold of yourself." He sobbed even louder. "Heck with it," I said, and started to go back into the Pyramid.

"Wait," yelled Ronnie, and at the same time there was a crash of glass in front of me.

"Oh, great," I said, as I saw the Mummy's hand scrabbling around the corner, dust puffing up around its wrapped fingers.

I started to run back toward Ronnie. "Ronnie, go that way. You have to exit," I said, pointing back towards Rusty's Railroad. "Ronnie, you have to leave, now!" I ordered.

He wasn't paying any attention to me. He was looking over my shoulder, his jaw slack and his eyes glassy. I heard a roar behind me, and turned, trembling.

"Don't let it eat me," whispered Ronnie.

"Easy, boy," I said. I was looking into the nostril hole of the Tyrannosaurus Rex skeleton. "Easy," I said. I could easily have fit in the nostril, I thought. Its breath stank like rotten meat, and it peered at me with one huge pupil-less eye-socket. *This Tyrannosaur skeleton is almost complete*, my brain randomly told me, *missing only four bones in the entire skeleton*. It didn't appear to need them.

"Don't let it eat me," Ronnie said again.

The huge skeleton sniffed, and I leaped back, falling into the Dino-Dig sand and scraping my arms as I tripped over Ronnie. The Tyrannosaurus flinched, making strange creaking noises as it reared back.

"Run," I said to Ronnie, scrambling to my feet. I made two more steps before I tripped again, jamming my knee into the sand and twisting an ankle. "Ow," I said, as the dinosaur roared behind me.

I glanced back at Ronnie. He was still staring stupidly up at the giant creature. "Don't eat me," he implored the monster.

"Run, Ronnie!" I yelled again, but it was too late. The dinosaur snapped once and got Ronnie's arm, and while Ronnie was screaming about that, it snapped once more and bit poor Ronnie's head off. His screaming stopped abruptly, save for a brief gurgling sound like water spitting from a hose.

I suppose, all in all, that that was really all that could have been done about the situation. The panic ended with Ronnie's death, as the Mummy collapsed and all the insects fell to the ground and the giant Tyrannosaurus broke into a bunch of bones and clattered into the Dino-Dig sand. Also, the wax Astronaut on the third floor stopped chasing the manager, and on the second floor, they were able to round up most of the carousel animals and take them back to the ground level, though apparently one of the horses did get away, as we were never able to find it again.

After witnessing my bravery with the insects and then so close to the huge Tyrannosaur, the new girl agreed to go to lunch with me, so it wasn't entirely a tragedy. After all, when one thinks of what *could* have happened, had the Tyrannosaur not gotten to Ronnie so quickly...

Why, who knows? It could very well have spelled, "The End."

The Hypnotist

"**S**ir, you, yes, the gentleman looking at his watch."

David looked up from his watch, across the table with his drink, past his wife, her back turned to him, past her drink, her hand resting on the base of the glass, to the stage hypnotist, who was beckoning him with an odd little motion.

"I enjoy volunteers, sir," the hypnotist said, "I especially enjoy picking my volunteers. Come up here, sir, please."

Slightly annoyed, David glanced around the lounge, all eyes on him. He knew some of the faces, people he had chatted with already on the cruise. Embarrassed, he shook his head slightly at the hypnotist, who beckoned again, more firmly. Now his wife, Amy, was looking at him expectantly, so David stood up, not too quickly, and approached the small stage. "Put your heart into it, honey," she whispered behind him.

"Your name?" asked the hypnotist.

"David."

"David, don't enter trance please until you've come all the way to the center of stage." David, put off a bit by the man's commanding attitude, had no intention of entering 'trance.' He stopped well short of the hypnotist, slouched a bit, and slid his hands into his pockets, feeling distinctly uncomfortable. The hypnotist smiled as though unconcerned. He walked over to David, took his arm gently and led him to the center of the stage. Someone in the audience giggled, and David glanced sharply over. A woman was laughing with a man in the corner, not watching the stage. David looked quickly back at the hypnotist, to find him watching him with raised eyebrows.

"I'm sorry, what did you say?" he asked. The hypnotist shook his head gently, and David said, "I thought you said something."

"David, are you awake?" the hypnotist asked.

"Of course I'm awake," David said, and this time he could not hide the hint of irritation in his voice.

The hypnotist turned to the audience. "Ladies and gentlemen, note the classic resistance. David is not consciously aware of his desire to enter trance. Indeed, his consciousness may be uncomfortable, perhaps almost resenting what is felt to be intrusion." He took a few steps away from David, towards the audience. "Note, however, the relaxation of the shoulders, the dip of the neck. The breathing beginning to slow. There is no doubt that David's subconscious mind, the mind behind the mind, may indeed desire the trance state. Are you sure you are awake, David?"

David, feeling his breathing beginning to slow a bit, said quickly, "I think so, yes."

The hypnotist looked doubtful. "Then how is it you can feel your heartbeat?" Actually, David could feel his heartbeat, which he thought must be unusual. "Is it slowing, like your breathing?" The hypnotist looked ever so slightly concerned. "David, close your eyes."

David closed his eyes.

"We must never forget," said the hypnotist, "that the conscious mind, overwhelmingly present though it is, is simply a pale, foggy mirror of the subconscious mind, which lies beneath it, and all around it. It is the subconscious mind's constant energy that fuels our every waking thought. Now David, your conscious mind may focus on whatever it finds interesting, you have no need to focus on my voice. I will speak, and the subconscious mind will hear what I say to it, and the conscious mind has no need to pay attention any more."

David was beginning to suspect he was in trance. He still had his doubts; he was relatively sure he was not about to start barking like a dog or dancing like a ballerina. But he was not sure he could still say, of course I'm awake. He could feel his heartbeat very clearly, a little thump in the chest area, followed by a quick surge of warmth through the body and limbs. He was not sure he'd ever felt this sensation before, at very least not with such power. Thump, surge; thump, surge. It was almost painful. He could count them; 1, 2... 4... 7... Slowing more with each one. They were definitely getting farther apart. 15... 16. He thought, I don't want to do this anymore, and opened his eyes.

The hypnotist was standing next to him, looking him in the eye with a slight frown. "Thank you, David, you were an excellent subject." Turning to the audience, "Thank you, David," and the audience applauded.

David, feeling out of place, his heartbeat fading back

into the background, trudged back to his table. Amy was grinning, sitting forward in her chair. "Dammit," he said, sitting down, "what did I do up there?"

Amy laughed. "Honey, he didn't make you do anything up there, don't worry."

David was looking furtively around the room. Over in the corner was a man he had met two days earlier, an audio technician from Denver. Was his name Ritchie? Ryan? He couldn't remember. A bit further and to the other side was the family of four staying two doors down from him. The little girl was staring at him, so he looked away. He said again to Amy, "What did he have me do?"

Amy pushed his drink toward him. "Shhh, nothing. Don't worry about it, David." Her head jerked toward the stage, where the hypnotist was already walking another subject, a shy looking middle-aged woman, to the center. David bit his lip, sinking back into his chair. Amy turned away from him again, leaning her back slightly against the table.

The subject after David went under very easily, it seemed. Within two minutes she was balancing precariously on the toes of one foot while trying to reach an imaginary cupboard. He hoped his own demonstration had not been so quick. Surely it hadn't; he was beginning to believe he hadn't entered trance at all. Or, at least not done anything he was not aware of. Would this woman remember her delicate pose on one foot?

After the show Amy said, "Let's look at the stars over the waves, it'll be romantic." So he followed her to the deck, put an arm around her waist, kissed her shoulder and neck and then they were interrupted by the family of four from two doors down. The two children ran by, first the little girl who had been staring earlier, then the slightly older boy, yelling at her with a scowl on his face. Then the mother's voice, light and cheerful, "Oh, Amy, David, that was wonderful!"

Amy turned to her, pushing David away a little bit, smiling. "Hush, Lisa, he's embarrassed."

Lisa laughed and patted David on the arm. "But it was so cute. Just hilarious." At David's puzzled look she turned back to Amy with, "Does he not remember?" as Lisa's husband Roger came up with a hearty, "Hey Dave, how you feeling?"

"Will someone please tell me what ridiculous thing he had me do?" asked David, trying to smile through his frustration.

"Hey," said Roger, "it was nothing, you blew some kisses at your wife is all." He laughed as David blushed. "Tell you the truth, I just thought you were going along with it, I didn't think he really got you, but I guess you don't remember it?" David shook his head. "Crazy," said Roger. "Was that a personal request, Amy? I saw you chatting with the hypnotist before the show. That was very funny."

Amy looked a bit startled, then laughed. "Oh no, not a request. I guess it was his idea."

David once again was beginning to feel slightly distant. "Funny," he said, with a smile he hoped didn't look too forced. "Was a weird experience."

"The kids thought it was great," said Lisa, just as the boy came running up to her.

"Mommy, come see the hypnotizer, Angie found the

hypnotizer," so they all followed the boy down the deck to where, indeed, the hypnotist was showing Angie something with a deck of cards. Most likely a card trick, judging by the girl's skeptical expression.

David felt oddly shy in front of the hypnotist, as well as a remote distaste for the man he couldn't quite place. He seemed like a pleasant enough sort of person, but his eyes were perhaps a bit active for David's taste, and a bit too piercing sometimes in staring. Was he mocking him? If so, it was not overt.

The card trick, if that was what it was, appeared to be over, and now the hypnotist was repeatedly shuffling the deck with his left hand, his right hand held out in greeting. He shook hands all around, finishing with David, "David, yes? I'm Martin Embers, thanks so much for your help on stage." He seemed to be looking past David, over his ear a little, his grip strong at first, then fading as he let go a bit slowly for David's taste. "I hope you didn't feel too uncomfortable up there."

"No, not at all," said David politely. "It was an interesting experience."

"Yes, very nice," said the hypnotist. "Your wife assured me you would make an excellent subject."

David shot Amy a look, not at all sure what to make of that. "Well, I wasn't really expecting it, but it was fun," he said, at the same time as Lisa said, "Mr. Embers, how do you do it?" and the hypnotist turned to Lisa with a smile.

"Really, Mrs. Claiborne, I do very little, the subject does most of the work on his own. The subconscious is very powerful, much more powerful than we give it credit for."

"I would love to be hypnotized," said Lisa with a huge

smile, and Roger immediately jumped in with, "Oh, no, not tonight, it's late. We were just on our way back to the room."

Martin smiled. "Of course, it is late. I have another show tomorrow evening. If you're in attendance, I'd be happy to have you as a volunteer."

After the family had left, Amy and the hypnotist exchanged a few words about New Mexico, where they had both grown up. David, from Maine, was starting to feel a bit left out of the conversation when Martin said, "Please, we can sit here in the lounge here." The lounge was empty, not too large, and long couches lined the walls. They sat down, and the hypnotist said, "David, tell me, how does your heart feel," and immediately David could feel his heart pounding in his chest.

"It feels fine. It's going a bit fast," he said.

"You can feel it very clearly, yes?"

"Yes, I can."

"Each second, every passing second, you can hear it beating more and more, yes?"

"Yes."

"Relax, David, realize there's no reason to be agitated. There's nothing to worry about. Just relax and listen to your heart beat, with each passing second."

"Am I hypnotized?" David asked, and his ears registered Amy's low chuckle beside him, but took no note of it.

"You may be sinking further into trance even as we speak."

David was almost sure he was correct. His heartbeat was getting stronger, he could hear it in his ears and feel its tingle throughout his body. "Why are you hypnotizing me now?" he asked, and again he took no notice of Amy's laugh beside him.

"Now David," said the hypnotist, "there is no need to be concerned. There is no need to be anything but relaxed, simply relaxed and full of the sound of your heart beating as it slows. Indeed, your conscious mind can feel free to wander as it will, free of the desire to focus on my voice. In all that I say, your subconscious will hear me and be able to respond."

It was beginning to be difficult to understand Martin over the sound of his own beating heart, but still he was on some deep level confused and concerned. Why was he being hypnotized now? "Is this necessary?" he asked.

Martin smiled and said, "You can close your eyes at any time you wish."

David thought, It would be nice to close my eyes, but with an effort he kept them open, focused on the bridge of the hypnotist's nose. With surprise he realized his right eye had fallen closed. He willed it open. He felt Amy shift beside him.

"David, your beautiful wife Amy would like to ask you a question. Isn't she beautiful, David?"

"Yes, she is."

"Will you answer Amy's question, David?"

After a slight pause, "Yes." David turned his head to Amy, who smiled and brushed her hair off her forehead.

"What's the password on the account, honey?"

For a moment David was completely disoriented. "What account?" he asked.

Amy's brow furrowed and she frowned slightly and

David blinked slowly and almost didn't open his eyes. When he did, Amy was smiling again. "The Lieberman account, honey, it's okay."

David swung his head over to Martin, whose eyes were focused past him, over his shoulder. David looked there and saw nothing but a small crack in the wall. He could not, of course, give away the password on the Lieberman account to anyone; those millions didn't belong to him, and David was a scrupulously honest man. He looked back at the hypnotist, who now was regarding him with a slight smile. "David," he said, "Listen carefully, I think someone forgot to wind the clock. Each second seems to be getting longer and longer."

David glanced over at the grandfather clock in the corner. It was ticking, he could hear it ticking, but it did seem to be slowing down. He could hear it so clearly across the room. He looked over at Amy, who was putting a pen into her purse and standing up. "Do you hear the clock, Amy?" he said, closing his eyes. "Is it slowing down? Why didn't they wind the clock?"

Amy put a hand on his face and smiled. "Oh, David. This clock hasn't been wound in years, till today. But don't worry, honey, relax. Close your eyes and listen to the clock beating."

David closed his eyes. For a few seconds he could hear both the clock ticking and his heart, out of time with each other. Relax, he thought, its been so long since I got a chance to relax, and now his heart was beating with the clock, each turn of the pendulum sending a full rushing warmth coursing through his body. He wondered how he had never felt this before, to feel so in tune with time.

His breathing slowed, each passing second eased more tension from his muscles. He did not notice as his wife and the hypnotist left the room, as with his eyes closed he sat and listened to the clock tick its last tock.

The War Is Over

by Curt Cannon

"Look at me. Look into my eyes."

The man was still not awake, Vorak could tell that. Still, he repeated the order aloud. "Look at me." He knew, somewhere in the man's unconscious, the words would be heard. When the man awoke, he would already be in tune with the voice that commanded him, already be prepared to obey its words.

Vorak looked over at the computer monitor to his right. The brain patterns showed marked corpal spikes – the man would still be asleep for some time. The drug had barely entered the third stage. Theoretically, two more stages of complete unconsciousness remained.

Of course, this being the first test on an actual human being, Vorak was prepared for any sort of reaction.

The sound of the door behind him made him turn. "What is it?" he said curtly. His assistant, Janet, frowned at his tone but didn't cower.

"Senator Brady's here."

"What? You let him in?" Vorak rubbed through his beard at his clenched jaw. "Are you insane?"

"How could I avoid it?" Janet said, reasonably. "It was you who told him to come by this week."

"Well, I didn't mean today!" Vorak looked down at the man unconscious on the hospital bed. "The senator cannot find out about this man."

Janet shrugged. "I will let him know you'll be out in a moment." She exited.

I must remain completely calm, Vorak thought. Cheerful, even. The senator will be expecting excitement. But not anxiety. He took a few deep breaths, all the way down to the diaphragm. Once more, he looked at the monitor, still heavily spiking. He could leave the man for a few moments, at least. He would send Janet back immediately. She would know to alert him the moment the next stage was reached.

*****

"Don't get up, Senator, please," Vorak said, crossing the study to the small sofa to shake hands with the seated politician. "Good to see you, sir." Vorak had traded his lab coat for a smoking jacket and quickly combed his hair on the way down the hall. He had left it a ratty mess, but he didn't know that, imagining it smoothly shadowing his narrow skull.

"Dr. Vorak," the Senator nodded, acknowledging the little man. "I hope I'm not interrupting your work."

"Not at all, Senator," said Vorak. "I was studying." He blinked. "That is, research."

Senator Brady nodded. "Doctor, I have a meeting in a half hour, so I can't stay long."

"Time enough for a drink?" asked Vorak.

"Oh, excellent," said Brady. "Rum and Pepsi." He waited, as Vorak poured the drink and took a seat across the small corner table. "I've just come from a talk with General Kloth."

Vorak barely stopped the frown from appearing on his face. "How is the General, sir?"

"He wants to know when it can be ready."

"Sir," said Vorak, blinking. The Senator wasn't wasting any time. "A few days, at least. Ahead of schedule." He said the last with slight emphasis, noting the Senator's impatience. "It's just not quite ready for testing."

"I know, I know," said the Senator, sighing. "We're all anxious, is all."

"As am I, Senator," Vorak said, forcing a small smile.

The Senator leaned back, sipping his drink. "The General had some excellent news, I'm happy to say. We've captured Hilo."

Vorak coughed, shocked to the core. I can't let it show, he thought. "Excellent," he murmured.

The Senator nodded. "We're very close, Doctor. The war is almost over. This mad cult will be nothing without its leaders. Only the big one is left, and we'll find him soon enough."

Vorak's head was spinning. In his mind he pictured the man laying on the hospital bed in the other room, the man he had thought was Hilo Sport. "It will be good to stop the madness," he said.

The Senator finished his drink and stood. "As soon as it's ready, Doctor," he said, "Call me. Let us know."

"I will, Senator," promised Vorak.

*****

It will indeed be good for all the madness to end,

thought the Senator as he got into the limousine. Things could go back to the way they had been, fifteen years ago. The way they had been for two hundred years, since the first administration of the Vaccine.

We've captured Hilo Sport, thought the Senator, and we've captured Jason Whispers. Only the top dog remains.

He could not understand such animals. The world had been given absolute peace, a cessation of all violence. And madmen such as these would (somehow!) reject it, would, instead, themselves become butchers, killers of men, women, and children. And now there were thousands who avoided taking the Vaccine. He couldn't understand it. They would rather spend life in prison? Thousands of children, growing up in danger of themselves each day, the capacity for violence ready to take over their brains at any time. Encouraged into violence, even, by their own parents and role models.

It was strange for the Senator, himself Vaccinated, to understand such things. How could one person inflict pain on another? It almost made him pass out to think about it, but he felt no shame about that. *Anyone* would feel this way, that's why we had to program machines to fight this terrible war for us.

All because three madmen – three *animals* – had somehow un-Vaccinated themselves, taught others to do the same, and begun waging war on the rest of us.

Asleep, they called us. Hypnotized.

Killers, the Senator thought angrily. That's what I call *them*. He could think of no more disgusting term than that.

"You told me you could bring me Hilo Sport," Vorak confronted Janet.

"I did!" replied Janet, indignant.

"That's not Sport," fumed Vorak. "Who is it?"

"What?" Janet seemed as shocked as Vorak. "Of course that's Hilo Sport."

"Where did you get this man?" Vorak demanded. The monitor still showed the heavy spiking; in the back of his mind he noted that stage three was starting to last a bit longer than projected.

"You said you didn't want to know that," said Janet, then, seeing Vorak's anger growing, "He came from Hilo Sport's house, whoever he is. From Hilo Sport's bed." She crossed her arms defensively. "As far as I know, that *is* Hilo Sport. It's not like I've ever met the man."

"I was just told that the government has Hilo Sport in custody."

Janet was silent for a moment. Finally, she said, "Well, either they are wrong, or we are."

Stay calm, Vorak thought to himself. He could feel anxiety building. Being Vaccinated, he desired no physical release for his anger. Still, he could feel it settling into stress across his shoulders. Breathe deeply, he thought. "So this man comes from Hilo Sport's house," he said, "from his bed." He did not think Janet would lie. "How do you come to know where his house is?"

"You said you didn't want to know these things," Janet repeated. She had a pinched look to her nose; she, too, must be very anxious. She sighed, "If you must know, Hilo Sport is a cousin."

"You're related?" he said, stunned. He had difficulty reconciling Hilo Sport as a relation of Janet Saint-Heather, descended directly from Miles Saint-Heather, who developed the Vaccine.

"Hilo Sport is a Saint-Heather," Janet said. "The secret black sheep." If I hadn't betrayed him, she thought, someone else would have. "I don't know if that's him," she said, "I don't know what he looks like. But I know the one who brought him to me thought he brought me Sport. I'm *sure* of that."

"I know," Vorak said, "I know." On the monitor, the corpal spikes had begun lengthening slightly. Later than expected, the man who should have been Hilo Sport was about to enter stage four, the last stage of unconsciousness. "We have to find out who this man is," he said. His mind churned desperately.

The government thinks they have Hilo Sport, he thought. Either they are wrong, or they are right. Most likely, they are right. They *should* know, he thought. They have the VAPOR, the digital network interface that stored each citizen's DNA profile.

"The VAPOR," he said aloud. Janet's eyes widened.

He had used it before. Not for a DNA profile, or for anything that might be flagged. It had been merely out of curiosity. Senator Brady, whose account he had used, would have no idea. An idiot, that man, whose most private password was the same as the drug he had asked Vorak to develop. Spelled backwards. To confuse the geniuses, thought Vorak, smiling slightly.

On the hospital bed, the man's breathing had slowed and the monitor showed a lot of green in the limbic region.

"Stage four," he said. "Make sure he is locked down tight, he could be dangerous." Janet began checking the arm restraints, bands and ropes that held his arms tightly to the bed. At the same time, Vorak reached up and pulled a hair from the man's head. The man's face remained still, the motion on the monitor constant.

"You're going to use the VAPOR?" Janet said. "You can't use the VAPOR."

"We have to use it," he said. "We have to know who he is."

"What if he's somebody important?" Janet said. "If he is, you *know* it will be flagged."

"If it's someone important," Vorak reasoned, "then it's that much more important that we know." He shrugged. "It will be on Senator Brady's account," he said.

"At this location. You know they can trace it."

Vorak shrugged again, and held out to her the hair he had pulled from the man's head. "Profile this," he said, "and I'll check it against the VAPOR." She took it. "Hurry," he said. "He could wake at any time." He began pacing as she left the room, the anxiety making his hands shake and sweat bead on his forehead.

Does it matter who it is, he wondered? We could just put him back, whoever he is. He shook his head. No, that wouldn't work at all. They had already given him the drug. He must be here when he awakes. I have to see it, I have to control it, Vorak thought. It's a delicate balance. His mind must be carefully realigned if he is to serve our purposes.

Besides, he thought, there's no time.

"I have it," Janet said, coming back into the room.

"Here." She handed him a tiny memory disk. He took it and slid it into the computer tower.

"Here goes," said Vorak. He typed one address and clicked four links and there it was: "VAPOR – Federal Login." Beneath that were several prominent legal notices concerning tampering and fraud. It's possible, he thought, that anyone who even accesses this login is flagged. Still, he told himself, it's not like you haven't done this before.

His fingers trembling, he typed, "Brady," then entered the Senator's social code, long memorized. Finally, the password. "Messiah," he said aloud, code-name of Vaccine-24.9, the drug they had injected into the man on the table. He typed it, backwards: "H-A-I-S-S-E-M."

"I'm in," he said. "Let me upload it." He navigated the menu, and shortly stood up, stepping back from the computer. "It will take a few seconds," he said. A small icon of an hourglass rotated on the screen. The sight irritated him; instead, he watched the man on the table. His eyes appeared to be moving rapidly beneath the closed lids. Stage 5 is coming any time, he thought. We must be ready.

The computer made a small dinging sound, and he heard Janet, watching the screen, gasp. He looked past her to the name that had appeared on the screen:

ELLIOTT WIM

"I don't understand," Vorak said aloud. "How is this possible?"

"He's the craziest of them all," Janet whispered.

How is this possible, Vorak thought, his mind in a whirl. All three are captured, and somehow, we have gotten the maddest of them all. Now when he looked at the man's face, his stomach lurched in revulsion. Elliott Wim. Vaccinated, but apparently it didn't take. Murderer with his bare hands. A biological impossibility. Even the other two of the revolutionary trio, Vaccinated, were incapable of murder.

But Elliott Wim.

"They say he does magic," Janet whispered.

"He's their leader," Vorak said. "Their legends can't be believed." Another thought hit him. "We've definitely been flagged. Have to have been. As soon as we uploaded the profile, no doubt. Get out of here," he told her. "They don't need to know you've been here." They'll be coming any time, he thought. Perhaps, with me, it won't matter. They need me, for the drug, he thought. But best to keep Janet safe. "Go," he told her.

She tried to object, but he didn't let her. "Trust me," he said, "I will work this to my advantage." He always had been capable of that. She left, and he sat and waited for the authorities, or for Elliott Wim to awake, whichever came first.

*****

Elliott was dreaming of cages. If it were someone else's dream, more notice might have been taken of the creatures in the cages, but to Elliott they were merely monstrous beasts. If it were another person's dream, that person might have said, "I dreamed of a zoo," and it did appear to be that. But for Elliott it was "cages," for Elliott, who remembered all his dreams very vividly, had decided cages represented the Vaccine, and so he loathed cages.

With a passion that, no doubt, inspired dream after dream.

All of Elliott's dreams were about cages.

This one was highly unusual, not in any particular sense, but simply because he couldn't control it. Normally, Elliott was a lucid dreamer, a trick he'd developed as a teen that allowed him to manipulate his dreams to varying degrees, sometimes with total control. Now, though he recognized himself to be dreaming, nothing was changing as he wished it to.

I've had this dream before, he thought. This is the one where I unlock the cages. That was the key. He understood the monsters were meant to frighten him. He recognized the impulse to run wildly through the maze, screaming, but he resisted, normally, because he recognized, it's about the cages.

Unlock the cages, he thought. That's all you have to do.

But not this time. Instead, this time, he ran wildly, screaming, all the while looking at himself as though he were someone else riding in this screaming body.

"Unlock the cages," he tried to say aloud, but the body kept running, kept screaming.

It's something they've done to me, he thought.

He remembered now, vaguely, being taken. He hadn't known, exactly, why he had gone to Hilo's that night; an intuition, strong, and he had trusted it. Now, it appeared, it had betrayed him. It was a bitter disappointment, but he accepted it. Live by the sword, die by the sword. That which you trust will always let you down, all things turn one way, then another in the end. They had come, thieves in the night, looking for Hilo, no doubt. Perhaps my intuition was for Hilo, he thought. By this switch he was saved.

It angered him, though, being taken. They have trapped me in this dream, he thought. They've caged me, he thought. In my own dream, I am caged. He trembled with anger.

*****

Vorak watched the body on the table, now shaking slightly, the eyes moving wildly. The line on the monitor was changing again, was beginning to flatten out.

He's beginning to enter stage five, Vorak thought. Behind him, he could hear a commotion. They'll try to break in, he thought. Let them. It will be men, not machines. They won't harm me. I have to be here for this. Still, he got up quickly and locked the door to the lab before returning to his seat.

"Look at me," he said, preparing Wim with his voice. "Look into my eyes." He would be awake any second now.

*****

Elliott dreamed, still, running through the cages. But something was changing. The monsters in the cages had started looking at him in fear. He could smell burning. Fire, he thought, that's my own anger. He could see, now, the cages were burning.

Yes, he thought. Burn the cages. And he let them burn. He could hear animals screaming, and knew some were getting hurt in the flames. I should unlock the cages, he thought. He unlocked one, two. The beast in the second cage rushed at him, a huge thing with claws, who swung and cut deeply into his arm. Elliott screamed, with pain

93

and anger. The whole dream was burning.

The cages, thought Elliott. Burn the cages.

*****

Stage five, thought Vorak. It has come. He is opening his eyes.

"Look at me, Elliott," he said. "Look into my eyes."

Elliott's eyes opened, and for a moment Vorak was confused. His eyes are glowing, he thought. What does that mean? Why would the drug make his eyes glow?

Then he thought, that's me. That's in my own mind. I'm hallucinating that his eyes are glowing. I've gone crazy. In Vorak's mind, it came out as a question. I've gone crazy?

He heard the men outside, now trying to break into the inner lab. They were shouting at him, but he ignored them.

Something has gone wrong, he thought, looking at the eyes of Elliott Wim. The drug has messed up, Messiah has failed.

Elliott was looking at him steadily, without expression. He looked down at his wrapped arms on the table, then back up at Vorak.

"Let me loose," he said. "I have work to do."

And Vorak, having gone mad, followed Wim's demand.

Dr. Blüdt

by Curt Cannon

Ben said, "What is this guy, German?" and Gary just shrugged his shoulders. He didn't know.

Ben said, "How do you pronounce that, anyway? Like, Blyoot? What?"

Gary did know that one. He said, "The lady I called said it just like 'blood.'"

"What, like, Dr. Blood?"

Gary nodded. "Yeah, except now that I think about it, the d at the end was a little bit harder, maybe halfway between a d and a t."

"That's kind of freaky. Dr. Blood."

"You think that's weird, take a look at the receptionist, I swear she's got fangs."

"No way."

"Yeah, seriously, take a look."

"I will." Ben straightened up a little bit, watching the receptionist, trying not to be obvious about it. He scooted over in his chair, this way a little bit, then that way. He said, "I don't see any fangs."

Gary shrugged. "Maybe you need a closer look. Why don't you go ask to borrow a pen or something, take a look then."

"She doesn't have fangs."

Gary said, "Okay. They aren't fangs. But they were kind of pointy. Just a little bit." He ran his tongue over his own teeth, thinking, mine are a little bit sharp, too. Maybe I have fangs.

Ben picked up a magazine and started flipping through it. Gary tried to get comfortable in his chair, not succeeding very well. He glanced at his watch. He wondered why you always had to wait so long for doctors.

Other than Gary and Ben, there was only one other person in the waiting room, a cute brunette on a cellular phone. She was wearing a tank top and jean shorts, tan leg showing up to the middle of the thigh. Ben could hear her half of the conversation. She was saying, "No... Yeah... No, I heard that from Amy. That's not what it was, though." She glanced up, saw him looking at her. He smiled, she smiled back. He was looking at her teeth, to see how sharp they were. They weren't. They were just straight, white, nice teeth. A nice smile.

She said, into the phone, "This guy is staring at me." Gary smiled a little more. She said, "Yeah, he is. He's got good eyes."

Ben nudged Gary with his elbow, saying, "Why don't you tell her about your hemorrhoids." Gary could've strangled him, but Ben hadn't said it very loud. Maybe she hadn't heard. He blushed, but the girl was still smiling at him. So he was still smiling back, though with less confidence.

She said, "I don't know. He's got a friend with him... Yeah, he is, too." Now Ben was grinning at the girl, looking sideways at Gary with mocking challenge. Gary thought, screw it, shook his head, picked up the *Discover* magazine Ben had set aside. But when the receptionist said "Cory Richards" and the girl stood up, he watched her leg out of the room. He said "Cory" to himself and filed the name away. Not that he'd ever see the girl again, most likely, but still.

Ben said, "You're right, they are kind of pointy."

"What?"

"The receptionist's teeth. They are kind of pointy. Not what I would really call fangs, but I guess you could make a case for it."

Gary said, "Oh."

Ben said, "What, you mad at me now? Don't like competition?"

Gary gave him a cold look and shook the magazine. "'Scuse me, I'm trying to read this article."

"Whatever."

They didn't speak to each other again until Gary's name got called, when Ben said, "That's you," and Gary said, "I know who I am, thanks." The receptionist's name, according to her name tag, was Darcy. He went back with her, trying not to walk funny. Had to be hemorrhoids, he knew what it was. He didn't even know why he was going to get it checked. Didn't they have over-the-counter stuff for that? But better safe than sorry, he supposed.

Darcy said, "Step up here." He stepped up. She measured his height and his weight. He stepped down. Darcy said, "Step in here, Dr. Blüdt will be with you in a moment." He stepped in, sat on the paper covered patient's chair, and waited.

And waited. And waited. He traced the bunnies on the

97

wallpaper all around the room, then started on the teddy bears. But they weren't quite continuous, like the bunnies were. He was trying to figure out how that could work when Dr. Blüdt came in.

He was a little on the plump side, red cheeks, rough skin. He didn't seem that old, but his hair was starting to go gray. Gary didn't think he looked German. Dutch, maybe, if you were really stretching for something European. He had a narrow nose fit in the middle of a florid face, and Gary thought, yeah, maybe the nose is Dutch.

Dr. Blüdt looked up from the clipboard he was carrying and said, "Gary Dermont?"

"Yes."

"It says here you've been experiencing, let me see, 'rectal pain, discomfort, and bleeding?'"

He did have a little bit of an accent, Gary decided, but he couldn't place it. Gary said, "Yes, sir."

Dr. Blüdt crinkled his forehead at him, frowning. He pulled a chair over, sat in it. He seemed to disapprove of something. He cleared his throat, shook his head, said, "I'll need to ask you a few questions." Gary said that was okay. Blüdt looked down at his papers, cleared his throat again, said, "It says here your blood type is O negative."

Gary said, "Yeah, I think that's right."

Dr. Blüdt said "hmmm" a few times and tapped his bottom lip with his index finger. He stood up and walked around Gary, looking him over. Gary tried not to fidget. Dr. Blüdt came back to the front, said, "Could you take off your shirt, please?"

Gary slid his shirt off, sucking in his stomach. Dr.

Blüdt lifted the stethoscope he had hanging around his neck and put it on his ears. He said, "This may be slightly cold, yes?" and touched it to Gary's chest.

It wasn't cold at all, though. It was almost uncomfortably hot. Dr. Blüdt held it in one place, till just before Gary thought it would actually burn him, then moved it to another spot. Dr. Blüdt said, "Breathe in, slowly, please," and Gary breathed in. Dr. Blüdt said, "Breathe out, slowly, please," and Gary breathed out.

Dr. Blüdt took the stethoscope off Gary's chest and moved it to his back. He said, "Breathe in, slowly, please," and Gary breathed in.

Dr. Blüdt held it too long this time, though, and when it started to burn, Gary said, "Ow!"

Dr. Blüdt pulled it away, said, "Too cold?"

Gary said, "No, too hot."

The doctor frowned, looking down at the stethoscope. "Hot?" Gary nodded. Dr. Blüdt said, "I have never heard of such a thing." He took two fingers and put them against the stethoscope's surface. He said, "To me it feels very cold. You are sure it's hot?" Gary nodded again, and the doctor's eyebrows came down in a frown. He said, "Well, no matter. You have a very healthy heart, very strong. Very capable. Yes?"

Gary said, "I guess so."

Dr. Blüdt said, "Very strong, very full, yes?" and took the stethoscope off his ears. He went to the door, said, "Wait, please. I will be back in a moment." He stepped out, the door shutting softly behind him.

Gary sat there, thinking, *What about my rectal pain, discomfort, and bleeding?* His back still hurt where the stethoscope had been, and he twisted his body, trying to see it. He couldn't see much of his back at all. He went to the mirror by the cabinet, looking over his shoulder at his back. There were two marks there, side by side, small vertical puffs of red. They didn't look much like the shape of the stethoscope, but there was no doubt they were right where the stethoscope had burned him.

He went back to the patient's chair, sat down. Ten minutes passed, or fifteen. The burn settled into a slight itch. The room was slightly chilly, and Gary pulled his shirt back on.

The door opened and Dr. Blüdt came back in. The stethoscope was gone from his neck. He had, in his right hand, a very large syringe and needle. Huge. Gary looked at it, thinking, *Don't let that be for my hemorrhoids.*

Dr. Blüdt said, "We must take some of your blood."

And Gary said, "What?"

Dr. Blüdt said, "We must, I'm afraid, take some of your blood."

"Why?" asked Gary, thinking, *With that huge thing? I won't have any blood left.*

"It is for your health?" He took Gary's arm, pushed the sleeve up, said, "Your hand, make a fist, please." Gary made a fist, the vein in his arm rising from the skin. Dr. Blüdt said, "Yes, yes. That is perfect. Very strong. Keep doing that, please." He went over to the cabinet, took out a bottle and a cotton ball, applied the bottle to the cotton ball, came back and swabbed Gary's exposed vein with the cotton ball. Said, "Yes, very good. Very healthy." He lofted the cotton ball toward the trash can, missing badly.

The doctor took the giant syringe in hand, looked at the

tip of the needle in the light. He said, "This may hurt a little bit," and, quickly, slid it into the vein.

Gary, though usually unaffected by needles, almost screamed. It more than hurt, the needle burned all the way up his arm. He gritted his teeth, bit his tongue, his eyes watering. It felt like the needle was growing, sliding up and up and up into his arm. He said, "Arghhh," strangling on it.

Dr. Blüdt glanced at him, his eyes bright. "It will hurt, only for a moment." Gary looked down at the syringe. It was filling quickly, making him dizzy just looking at it. He closed his eyes. A moment later, he felt the needle slide out, the pain shooting sharply through his arm again, then suddenly gone. He opened his eyes.

Dr. Blüdt was already across the room, by the sink. His back was to Gary, hiding whatever he was doing. Gary looked down at his arm. It was bleeding, red trickling down the crease on either side of his elbow. He said, "Hey, you have a Band-Aid?" Dr. Blüdt didn't hear him, or ignored him. Gary put his index finger over the hole in his arm, trying use his thumb to wipe the already spilled blood away. It did nothing to clean up the blood, only leaving long red streaks along his bicep.

Dr. Blüdt turned around, came back over. He held up Gary's syringe. It was blood-streaked but empty. The doctor shrugged his shoulders, said, "I am sorry, I was very careless. Your blood spilled, yes? All over, into the sink."

Gary said, "What?"

"We must do it again, yes?"

Gary said, "What? With that thing?"

101

Dr. Blüdt said, "No, no. It is very unsanitary. I have another." He reached into his white coat pocket and pulled out another syringe, even bigger than the first.

Gary said, "Are you crazy?"

Blüdt frowned deeply. "It is for your health, yes?" He grabbed Gary's arm, pulled Gary's finger away from the wound. He said, "Make a fist, please." Gary didn't, just looking at him. The doctor said, "Please. It is for your health, yes." Gary frowned, reluctantly making a fist. Dr. Blüdt said, "Yes, good. Hold that, please," and went back to the cabinets. He repeated the cotton-ball procedure. When he was done swabbing the vein, he said, "This may hurt, a very little bit."

Gary said, "Yeah?" And then screamed. His whole body tensed as the needle glided into his arm and grew and spread out up his neck and across his back and through his shoulders and down to his toes. He said, "Aaah!" He said, "Whuh!" He said, "Pleeeeeeeeease!"

The needle slid out. Dr. Blüdt said, "That was not so bad, no?"

Gary opened his eyes, gasping. Dr. Blüdt was across the room again, his back to Gary. Gary said, between breaths, "Hey, don't... Don't spill... Don't spill this one... Okay?" He looked down at his arm. There was blood all over it. He said, "Whoa." There were two holes in his arm now, right next to each other.

Gary said, "Hey, I really need a —" and would have said "Band-Aid," but at that moment the door burst open and a big black man came in. In his right hand was a sharp wooden stake, in his left hand was a bow, and strapped to his back was a quarrel of arrows and what looked like a

102

wooden sword.

The doctor turned around. He was still holding the syringe in his hand. His face was red, stained, his lips dark with blood.

Gary said, "What?!"

The black man said, "Dr. Blüdt!"

Dr. Blüdt said, "You!"

The black man leaped forward, the hand with the bow trailing behind him, the hand with the stake swinging at the doctor. Blüdt dodged aside. The stake brushed by him, crashing into the sink, breaking in half. The black man grunted, tripping, his shoulder ramming into the wall.

Gary said, "What?"

Dr. Blüdt was by the cabinets, pulling open drawers. The needle was still in his left hand. He slammed a drawer shut, switched the syringe to his right hand, raising it and turning to face the black man. The black man drew his sword and flung it at the doctor. Blüdt ducked, the sword sailing over his head. The black man drew an arrow, cocked it. Dr. Blüdt screamed. Gary screamed. The black man said, "Aiyh!" The bow twanged, Dr. Blüdt crashed back into the cabinets, the arrow sticking out of his chest.

Gary said, "What? What?"

The black man slung his bow over his shoulder. He stepped over to Blüdt, looking at his face, touching it. He picked up his sword and sheathed it at his back.

Gary said, "What?"

The black man said, "Are you all right?"

Gary said, "What?"

The man held out his hand and said, "Kenny, Vampire Slayer. I've been after this one for a while."

Gary said, "What?"

Kenny the Vampire Slayer said, "I can understand, you're a little confused, a little startled. Just stay calm, it's taken care of."

Gary said, "What the?"

Kenny said, "Don't worry." He went over to the counter by the sink. Picked up the clipboard sitting there, looked at it, said, "Gary Dermont?" Gary could only nod. Kenny looked the chart over, said, "Hmmm. Almost definitely hemorrhoids. You think it's hemorrhoids?"

Gary said, "What?"

Kenny took out a pen, flipped back a few pages in the clipboard. He started scribbling something. He said, "I'm writing you out a prescription for some hydrocortisone cream, you take it to the drugstore, it'll come with application instructions."

Gary said, "What?"

Kenny looked at him over the clipboard, said, "Don't worry, I'm a doctor." He tore out the prescription and handed it to Gary. Gary took it, his hand shaking. Kenny said, "I could inspect you, make sure, if you want?"

Gary said, "What? Uh, no, that's okay."

Kenny said, "Okay. You all right? You can go ahead on out. I've got some stuff to take care of back here. Don't worry about paying... The receptionist was one of these, too." He pointed at Dr. Blüdt.

Gary said, "Yeah... I thought..." —had to clear his throat— "I thought so."

Kenny kneeled down by Dr. Blüdt, and Gary walked out. He took a wrong turn, came back, looked for the scale, and followed it to the waiting room. Ben was still sitting there, reading *Discover*, like nothing had happened. Ben looked up, said, "Hemorrhoids?" Gary nodded. Ben said, frowning, "You have blood all over your arm."

Gary said, "Yeah, I had to give some blood."

Ben said, "They didn't give you a Band-Aid."

Gary said, "Nope."

Ben said, "Probably only had those Mickey Mouse ones or something, anyway." He put the *Discover* down, stood up, said, "You got a prescription?" Gary nodded. Ben nodded. Ben said, "Okay, then. Let's go pick it up."

Eden

by Luke Everett

I.

The sun was there first, soft through her lashes, then the blue of sky and light clouds, pure white and streaking across the sky. Then the world was around her. Grass was soft under her back, trees were tall on the edges of her vision. She was naked, and vaguely ashamed. A breeze blew, soft on her face, with the scent of almonds. She was no longer ashamed.

She turned her head, and a man was there, also naked. He was looking at her, his eyes damp and thoughtful. He is beautiful, she thought, and said, "You are beautiful."

He smiled, that beautiful as well. He said, "Thank you," and, "You are awake."

She nodded, sitting up. The grass was gentle, without itch or flaw, and she rested her fingers in it, weaving them together. She felt her eyes widen, taking in flowers bigger and brighter than she had ever seen, a stream, and animals, unafraid, resting near them. She said, "This is the most beautiful day I have ever seen."

He nodded, agreeing, then saying, "Have you ever seen another?"

She thought, and could not remember that she had.

He said, "Walk with me." She stood, and they walked through the forest. Soon their hands were joined, and later, when night came, their bodies. She fell asleep with her back against his chest and his hand on her stomach and felt content.

But she dreamed:

In the sky a great cloud was everywhere, and the sky was black. It was day, but the sun was dark and dull, a disc of tarnished metal high in the sky. There were people, thousands of them. They were running and screaming, and they covered their nakedness with leaves, ashamed.

Overhead, beneath the great cloud, black birds circled. Or they were silver, but the dark made them shadows. They circled, then came swooping from the sky, shrieking. And they spoke, in dry unforgiving tones.

She ran, as the others did, screaming. But a man grabbed her arm and stopped her, looked in her eyes. His were distant blue and without emotion. He said, "Do not be afraid." He took her hand gently, and she felt his fingers in her own. They were hard, plastic.

She awoke then, chilled and sweating, her lover's hand still gently below her breast. She clutched it in her own, desperately, whispering, "Stephen."

A breeze blew with the scent of almonds, and she remembered, he had no name, or none that he had told her. She too was nameless. But she said it again, "Stephen? Hold me, Stephen."

The wind grew stronger around her, the scent stronger, and she became afraid. It blew against her face, strong enough to steal her breath, leave her gasping. "Help me,

Stephen," she said, but he slept on. She turned, looked at his peaceful sleep. His breath was gentle and undisturbed by the wind that tore around them. His hair was undisturbed and motionless on his head. And hers, too, undisturbed on his shoulder. "Oh, Stephen," she said, and began to cry. The wind whipped around her, almond filled her nose. The world faded away.

II.

The sun was there, then the blue sky and streaks of cloud. She traced one with her eyes to where it joined another. *Lion*, she thought, for that was the tail, and that the body, and there was the mane. And then, from a gaping mouth, little puffs of white trailing away. *It's the roar*, she thought, and giggled.

"You are awake," she heard, and she turned her head. A man was sitting there, naked like herself. She had never seen him before. He said, "You are beautiful."

She nodded, because she knew this was true. He was beautiful too, as was everything. She sat up. The grass was gentle, without itch or flaw. She brushed her hair away from her face. Her hand passed in front of her eyes, and she stared at it, fascinated. The fingers were long and delicate. The nails were short and jagged. She remembered them longer, and sometimes red. Bright red, shiny red.

The man beside her stood. "Walk with me," he said, and she nodded. But walking did not seem right, somehow. She wanted to run. She said, *Run with me*, but she didn't say it, she realized. Her mouth was closed. Her eyes were closed. She was crying. He said, "What's the matter?" She said, *This. Everything.* But still she said

109

nothing. He said, "Claudia?" But that wasn't her name, and she saw in his face when he realized that. His mouth opened but was silent, like hers. They stared at each other in that silence.

She turned and ran from him, into the forest. Faster and faster she ran. She heard him behind her, following, but she kept her face forward, into the wind. Tears streamed back to her temples. The wind blew around her, tore at her, a wind full of the fragrance of almond. She found the odor frightening. She remembered it vaguely, so vaguely.

She stopped suddenly, turning, and the man crashed into her, knocking her to the ground. "I'm sorry," he whispered, "Please, I'm sorry." He lifted her in strong arms, carrying her back the way they had come. She turned her face into his chest, a smooth and scentless wall between herself and fear.

*****

"What were you running from?" he asked her later. But she was silent, still. She was incapable of speech, she had discovered. He said, "Is it me?" But of course it wasn't him, he was beautiful. He was perfect. Or perhaps it *was* him; perhaps there was something missing in him, in his eyes, his voice, something she could remember seeing once out of the corner of her eyes... but not in this place, or this time. And not with this man.

She wanted to say, *Where am I? Where are we?* But she thought he wouldn't know, or even care. Is that what was missing? A sense of identity? Of purpose? She knew nothing of herself, or of him. Perhaps there was nothing to know; perhaps they were born here, of the earth and the sky and the sun, without past, as they were. Perfect, both of them.

He was still looking at her, apprehensive. "Is it me?" he asked again. She shook her head, forced a smile. She took him into her arms. He needed her, she decided. She didn't need him. But she needed something.

*****

Her sleep that night was dreamless. She slipped awake, into a cool wind, and realized she was speaking. Meaningless words, or words she didn't know, but her voice was there. She looked at him, still sleeping. "Wake up," she said, but he didn't. She left him there and made her way into the forest, still dim in the morning sun. She came back to him, and he was awake, watching her.

"Who is Claudia?" she asked, curious.

"I don't know what you mean," he said, and she could tell he didn't.

She sat next to him and took his hand in her lap. "What's your name?" she said.

"Do we have names?" he asked.

She didn't know. She wanted one. She said, "Call me Claudia."

He called her that. She was Claudia for that day. But that night, their bodies joined, and "Claudia," he said... Then, "Claudia?" And then he stopped, became still. A breeze blew and chilled them in their sweat. He shivered. He pulled away from her, stood up. He was crying. He said, "Stop that."

"What?" she said.

He said, "Stop that," but he wasn't looking at her, he was looking over her shoulder. She turned around, but there was nothing there. He said, "Stop that, go away. I can't."

"Can't what?"

"Stop that. Please... I am not me, I can't."

She realized it then, that she, too, was not herself. She said, "I am not me." It was a revelation. "I am not this." But then wind was growing, and the scent of almond. But she realized, too, this wasn't real wind, or real almond. She said, "Stephen, this isn't real."

He said, "I am not Stephen."

"You must be," she said, "You must." But her breath by then was going, and the world was starting to fragment. She slid one way, and he another, and the world slid down and down and down.

III.

And she woke up floating, feeling nothing, staring into darkness. So dark she had to ask herself if her eyes were open. But were they? She couldn't tell. She had to ask herself, *Do I exist?* She saw nothing, heard nothing, felt nothing... not her hands, her feet... not her breathing... no expression on her face.

I am dead, she thought. This was purgatory, or hell. Or the inside of a coffin when the spirit diffuses. *I am dead.* And she thought of that, and dwelt on it, and considered it, for hours and days and years on end.

IV.

Until, quite suddenly, she is nineteen again, but it isn't

again, it's now. And yes, she remembers it, some... but no, this is *it.*

And she is at a party with Rachel, and she's drinking a little too much, maybe, and she's looking at a guy across the room and thinking maybe she's seen him on TV. She grabs Rachel's arm, says, "That guy over there, who is he?"

Rachel turns, brushes her eyes over that corner, "Who? I don't know them."

"That guy right there, I think I've seen him on TV." And then, for a flash of a second, her heart stops and her breathing stops, he's glanced this way and somehow their eyes have met. Did he smile? She isn't sure. She is afraid she didn't, but she hadn't had time. And now her heart is beating double, too fast, and she has to take another drink.

Rachel says, "Hey, look, it's Vick," and leaves her standing by herself. She doesn't want to follow, she wants to get another rum and coke, or really anything the least bit mind-affecting. She turns and heads back to the counter, and she bumps into him then, the sneaky bastard is behind her. He has his TV confidence turned on, that air she had recognized across the room. He has a lopsided smile.

"Hi," he says, "I'm Eric."

V.

Almond, and she is twenty-three. She's in a plane, seat 26-A, looking out the window at the runway. This is it, the big move of her life, the time has come, the future is now. The seat next to her is empty, and she hopes it stays that way. But there are people filing in now... old woman, passing... a frazzled Mom with a fat bully-looking kid, passing (thank God)... a thug, about her age, in a basketball jersey, earring, tattoo, not passing... Damn.

"This 26?" he asks, as though it's not obvious. She starts to pack her carry-on in tighter, he says, "Hey, no problem, there's lots of room." He stuffs his gym bag down under the seat. He settles in, leans his head back, closes his eyes, maybe he'll sleep. She hopes. But then, a bit later, he opens his eyes, and she realizes she's been watching the whole time, because when they open, right there, they are looking at each other. He has soft brown eyes, almost amber in the warm light of the plane. And he looks away, just for a second, and he looks back with this tiny little shy smile and she realizes, unexpectedly, she is hooked, just like that. Embarrassed, she turns, stares back out at the runway. He says, "Hey, I'm sorry, I'm not bothering you, am I?"

She says, "No, of course not," but he is. Because now she doesn't know how to act, she doesn't know what happened. She can't turn around and look at him. She says, to fill the silence, "I'm moving, I just got a job in New York."

He says, "You're from here?"

"Yeah."

"Are you scared, excited, what?"

"I don't know, both, I guess." She wants to turn back around now, see what he looks like again. But somehow it's easier to watch the slight bit of reflection in the window. She says, "It's not the first time I've gone away, you know, college, I did that. But this is a little scarier, I

114

don't know. School, you have counselors and teachers and grades and you know everything you're doing. Now I'll be just... on my own."

He says, "What will you be doing? The job, I mean."

"For a theater, props manager. You know, I call places, get stuff, figure out what they need for things, that kind of thing."

"Theater in New York, that's a big deal." And he sounds like he means it, even.

She says, "Yeah, it is, I guess." She glances back at him and he is smiling at her, attentive. Somehow she doesn't want this conversation to slip away. She says, "You going to New York?"

He shakes his head, "No, New York's okay, but all the people, big buildings. Gives me a headache. My Dad, he lives in Newark, he's a doctor, does research up there, I'm going up to be his personal assistant. I think I'll like it, you know?" He looks a little self-conscious now, with her looking at him, but she can't help it. His fingers are toying with his ear-ring. He says, "He's a neurologist, does brain stuff. Like experiments. He was telling me, on the phone... they can open up a guy's head, put electrodes down, and if you put a little current through you can pretty much completely control a guy's thoughts. I guess that's the theory anyway, I mean, they can't control it completely yet, they don't really know all that much about the brain. But for instance... you put a wire in one particular spot, hit the buzzer, and the guy remembers when he was four years old, in detail, you know? Like he's four again. Or you put it another place and he'll taste coffee. Weird stuff. One guy, didn't matter where they put it, or what it did, every time they did it he'd see a butterfly. You know, he might jump back in time, or he might taste coffee, or whatever, but he'd still see that butterfly flying around. Makes you wonder."

But she is not paying attention anymore. She is thinking, thinking hard, but about what? That's the trouble, she doesn't know. He has confused her. She shakes her head, clears it. They talk, the rest of the flight, and as they're touching down, he says, "Hey." He looks nervous. He has his napkin and he writes on it, he says, "This is me, okay? Call me." And she looks at the napkin, with a number, and it's got a name. It says, "Michael."

And a gust of wind picks it up, blows it away.

VI.

She is twenty-five. A Tuesday afternoon, and she's in a hurry, because she has Wednesday and Thursday off and she's missing Mike. She's looking for an authentic truck. They're doing *Mama Had a Nightmare*, of all the horrible plays, and somebody had the bright idea of driving a damn vintage truck across stage midway through the second act (well after anybody really gives a damn), and she's got to find one before Friday. And Lorrie says Ryan says his friend Stacy's brother has a collection of old cars and trucks on Long Island.

Traffic is horrible. She is tired, angry. She should have listened to everyone who said, "Don't get a car in New York," but she was doing so *good*, out of the studio apartment and into something bigger, nicer, a window that actually looked out on a *parking lot*, of all things, and wouldn't it be nice if she could *drive* to pick up these things instead of relying on taxis and Lorrie and Harry and Nathan and Sammy's brother's cousin with the pickup.

And now she has a flat, of all the damn things. In the middle of the bridge, embarrassed, late, watching people slip by and eyeing her discomfort. And this is New York, right, and nobody will offer you help, and if they do, most likely you don't *want* whatever kind of help they're offering...

And who is this guy pulling up? He looks nice, he looks okay, but still... this is New York. And he's handsome, and clean cut, and in a suit. And he might be okay. And he's walking up.

"Hi," he says, "I'm Stephen, can I help?"

VII.

She is floating, staring into the black. She feels nothing, but she knows now, she is not dead. They have found something important, and everything will be good now. She is content, reassured. This is not death, this is birth, the world is reforming, she can feel her hands again, and her feet. An expression on her face.

And then the sun is there, the blue sky and streaks of cloud. The grass is soft, without itch or flaw. She is naked, but unashamed.

She turns her head, and a man is there, naked as well. He is looking at her, his eyes damp and thoughtful. He is beautiful, she thinks, and says to him, "You are beautiful."

He smiles, that beautiful as well. He reaches out, he touches her face. "Thank you," he tells her. "I am Stephen.

"You are Eve."

Blood Hungers

by Kyle Staples

Pete said, "Hey, wait... Wait, I think he's dead," but at first nobody paid any attention. They were flipping curses, having fun with it as they kicked the kid. Pete said again, "I think he's dead," and that time Ron heard him. Ron said, "No way," but stopped his kicking, and then Nick and Louis stopped too. They looked down at the unmoving boy.

Nick said, "What?" and Pete said, "He stopped moving, you guys don't see he stopped moving? I don't think he's breathing," and Ron said, "No fucking way," but it was Louis who got down by the kid and checked. He put his hand in front of the kid's mouth, then pressed his fingers against his neck. He shook his head a little bit, said, "Feels like he's dead," and then, "I got blood on my hand." That bothered Louis, which was why he was almost strictly a kicker. He'd let Ron and Pete and Nick start in with the punching, and he'd kick them once they were on the ground.

Louis stood up and wiped his hand on his jeans. Clean before, now they had a single dark streak just below the right pocket. They were all looking at each other, the body of the boy in the center of them. Pete said, "What the fuck did you guys do?"

Louis said, "Us?

Ron said, "I don't see how we could have killed him. I just hit him a little."

Louis said, "Man, all I did was kick his stomach a couple times."

"Guys, shut the fuck up." Nick kneeled down by the body, feeling around it.

"Should you touch it?" said Pete.

"We already touched him," Nick snapped.

"I mean should we touch him more?"

Nick stood up and glared at Pete. "Shut up, dammit, shut up, okay you fucking pansy?" They did. Only Ron, Nick's brother, ever much argued with Nick, but Ron looked as scared shitless as everyone else. Nick got down by the body and looked at it. "I think we busted his head too hard. Man, somebody got him in the temple." He stood up, shaking his head. "Fuck!" It was a quick, angry exclamation.

"We have to get rid of the body," said Nick. Ron stood up and started walking away. "Ron, get back here," yelled Nick, but Ron said, "Sorry guys, I'm out," and kept walking. Nick ran behind him, grabbed his shoulder and pulled him back, whispering something in his ear the others didn't hear. Ron, looking sullen, came back to where the others stood.

Louis asked, "Anyone know this kid?"

But he knew they didn't. They never knew the people they jumped; they were just looking for some fun, a little action, whoever walked their way. It was probably someone from school, but Louis didn't recognize him.

"I think he was in my science class," said Pete, and everyone looked at him.

"You *think*?" spat Nick. "What's his name?"

"I don't know, it was a big class and school was a month ago, man. I don't know him, okay?"

"We have to get rid of the body," Nick said again. "We have to get rid of the body, *now*." He paced the alley, absently rubbing his left cheek. They were in the shadows, certainly, but the street where they grabbed the kid was ten feet down, and there were houses on either side of the alley, both some distance away. On one side of the alley was a fence; its shadow obscured most of the body. One arm was flung out into the light, the hand closed into a fist. A ring glittered red in the setting sun.

"Why don't we just leave it here?" asked Pete, and Ron started nodding.

Nick was furious. "What the hell is wrong with you guys? How many people have we jumped here?" The correct answer was five, but nobody said anything. "You think people don't *know* what we do here?"

Ron said, "We've never gotten caught," and Nick started trembling he was so angry.

"If this body is found here we're all in deep shit. Deep shit!" He glared at each of them in turn. "You guys do whatever the fuck you want. I'm getting rid of this body because somebody has to and I guess that means it's going to be me." He leaned into the shadow of the fence and started to hoist the body up by the arms. Louis grabbed the legs, then dropped them suddenly and turned into the fence and vomited. He turned back and grabbed the legs again. Nick said, "Man, you all right?" and Louis nodded.

"Where are we taking him?"

"Down to the creek," said Nick, "maybe the underpass?"

"There's that old shed there," said Ron, "but how are we going to get it there?"

"My old man's probably sleeping," said Pete, "I can take the car." Pete's house was only a little ways down the block. "Be in some trouble if he finds out."

"You have to go get it," said Nick, "and hurry." Pete ran off down the alley. Nick said to Louis, "Help me drag it behind this bush till he gets back." So they pulled the body over behind a bush. The grass and weeds were bent where the body had been, and there was a little blood on the fence, but you had to get right up next to it to see it in the light. "Everybody don't stand so close," Nick said. They all backed up a little. "Don't look so guilty," he told them, so Ron put his hands in his pockets and Louis sat on the ground.

A few minutes later Pete pulled the car into the alley. No one had passed. Pete jumped out of the front seat and opened the back door. "I brought this blanket, don't get blood on the seats, please don't get blood on the seats."

"Are we putting him in the back seat," asked Louis, "or in the trunk?"

"Man, just hurry," said Nick, his hands shaking and sweat trickling down his cheek. They spread the blanket over the back seat and Ron and Pete hoisted the body onto the blanket. Nick slammed the car door shut. He turned to Pete and said, "Drive. I go with you."

"Where you going to put it?" asked Ron.

"Shut up," said Nick, walking around the car to the passenger side. "You two walk home, act regular, don't say anything ever." He got in the car, slammed the door, and watched Pete climb into the driver's seat. Louis started down the alley. Ron looked into the back seat of the car, glared at Nick, then turned to follow Louis.

Ron's house was past Louis's, in the same direction, but neither was very far. They didn't make it to Louis's house before he started crying. It was just a little bit at first. Ron didn't say anything. Then it turned into big wracking sobs. Ron gently said, "Geez, Louis, get a hold of yourself." Louis turned to him, crying harder, and leaned into him, and Ron had to catch him. Suddenly they were hugging in the middle of the sidewalk, with Louis bawling his eyes out. Ron said, "Louis, someone's going to see us."

Louis said, "Oh my God oh my God." He was sobbing too hard to say anything else.

Ron said, "Come on, Louis, stand up and we'll walk to my house, okay? Someone's going to see us."

Louis stood up and sniffed a couple times. "Right, all right. Yeah." They started walking down the street again. In a bit Louis had settled down and looked normal, except for puffy eyes. He said, "I don't know, Ronnie, I don't know about this." Ron didn't say anything. Louis walked a little more and said, "We have to completely forget about this."

Ron said, "Yeah? So get started."

Louis grunted, but he was beginning to feel better, and could tell Ron was starting to get irritated. "I'm sorry," he said, "Hey, I'm sorry. I'm just a little shook up."

"Me too," Ron said, "But you can't just act like a fool."

"I know," said Louis.

"Look," Ron said, "We can't talk about this, you know?"

"I know," said Louis."

"And Louis," said Ron, now stopping and talking very seriously, "Listen. You have to forget all this. And I don't mean so we don't get caught, but yes, so we don't get caught. But you need to leave this behind us. You know? You have to get over it. You have to *forget it.*"

Louis nodded. "I know."

Ron started walking again and Louis followed him. They didn't say anything until they had arrived at Ron's house, and Ron said, "Play some Playstation?" and Louis said, "Sure," and Ron started flipping through games. Louis sat down on the couch, leaning his head back. He was tired, drifting off. He said, "Man, you play, I'm gonna catch a short nap," and Ron said, "Okay, cool," and Louis drifted into sleep.

*****

When he woke up he was lying on his side on the couch and someone had put a little blanket over his legs. He kicked it off, stood up, and stretched. There was an opening to the kitchen on one side, but though he could hear Ron's family having dinner, he couldn't see into the kitchen through the wall that cut the two rooms in half.

He could hear Nick talking, and his whole body started to shake as he remembered what had happened. He sat back down on the couch, trying to be quiet, not wanting them to know he was awake. Nick said, "I just don't why we have to always be having people over, that's all." He sounded tense but not particularly angry.

"C'mon, Nicholas, it's Ron's friend." That was Ron's

124

mom, slightly pleading but mostly disinterested. But she was firm when she said, "Look, he's spending the night, Ron already asked before you got home, okay?"

There was no response, just the click of silverware on glass plates. Louis got up quietly and went upstairs to Ron's room. He shut the door, sat on the bed. He flipped through some comic books. He was getting a headache, bad.

After a while Ron came in. "Woke up, huh?" He said. Louis nodded, not looking up from *The Fantastic Four*. Ron said, "I'm so glad I don't have to work tomorrow, get to sleep in."

"Yeah," Louis nodded again. He closed the comic book and looked up at Ron. "Hey, what's up with your hair?" he said.

Ron looked confused. "What?"

Louis stood up and set the comic book down. "What is that?" He squinted. Ron kept flinching away. "Hey, stay still," Louis said, peering intently at Ron. "I thought your hair was frizzed out weird or something, but that's not what that is."

Ron said, "What what is?" He was starting to sound scared.

"Man, it looks like you're smoking. I mean, like you have smoke coming off you."

"Louis, shut up," Ron said. He pushed Louis away, kicked through some clothes over to a mirror, inspecting himself. "I don't see anything." He looked back at Louis. "Quit fucking with me."

Louis came over and stood behind him, looking into the mirror. He could see it clearly, even through the mirror, not *what* it was, true, but *that* it was. "You don't see that?"

"Fuck you," said Ron.

"That's weird," said Louis. "It's on me, too." He started looking at his arms and hands.

Ron scooped the *Fantastic Four* off the bed and sprawled out over the blankets. "Man, shut up." He opened the comic book somewhere in the middle, looking at the pictures. Louis had a pinched, concerned look on his face but didn't say anything.

Restless, Ron threw down the comic book and stood up. "I'm going up on the roof," he said. A segment of ledge outside Ron's window made it pretty easy to climb onto the roof of the house, and in the middle you could sit down between two sections of the roof and not be seen from the street. Ron pulled the blinds up on the window and pulled it open, stepping up and around and disappearing. After a moment, Louis followed him up to the little enclave, where Ron was lighting a joint.

Louis sat next to him, and Ron silently passed him the joint. Louis looked up at the stars and the crooked sliver of the moon as they passed the weed back and forth.

Not long later, Nick climbed up to join them. It was hard to gauge his mood in the darkness, but he sounded irritated when he said to Louis, "Man, why are you spending the night?"

Louis said, "What?"

Ron said, "Jesus, Nick, it would be strange if he didn't spend the night. And be quiet, you want Mom to know this place is up here?"

Nick lowered his voice to match their quiet tones. "Louis, you aren't freaking out, are you?" He sat down and took the joint. "Cause if you're freaking out, I'll kill you."

Ron said, "He's fine."

It was too dark to see if Nick had any of the strange smoke coming off of him. Quietly, Nick said, "Listen. We took it down to the shed by the underpass, but we thought about it more and we don't think that's good enough. It's too close. Tomorrow we're going to take it farther, out to Huntsville."

"Why didn't you take it there already?" Ron asked.

"Pete couldn't take the car that long."

Louis said, "Someone's going to find it in that shed."

"Overnight?" asked Nick. "We put it in plastic and covered it, I don't think so. And there's nothing right now that points it to us."

Ron shook his head. "Then why not just leave it."

Nick hesitated a long second. "It's too close, it's too much us. People know about that shed, you know that. I asked Mom if I could take the car to Brownsburg tomorrow, she knows I'm supposed to go see Andie anyway. I just think that's better."

Ron said, "What about Andie?"

Nick said, "She'll cover for me."

Ron said, "You're gonna tell her?"

Nick said, "Hell no. I'll tell her something else." That seemed to satisfy Ron. Nick had pretty much taken over the joint, but nobody said anything as he took a final hit and pinched it out. He stood up. "Look, we can't tell anyone anything about this, ever. I mean that. Wouldn't hurt for you guys to find something to do tomorrow, make yourselves a little visible. But that's it on talking about this. It's over and done. Got it?" They made little sounds of agreement, and Nick climbed back off the roof and disappeared.

Louis lay down on the incline of the roof, looking up at the stars again. He said, "I think he had that smoky stuff coming off of him, too."

Ron said, "Who, Nick?" Louis nodded. Ron said, "I don't know what you're talking about."

Louis said, "Never mind."

Ron said, "Yeah, you're starting to freak me out," and then he, too, got up and disappeared off the roof. Louis lay there, looking at the stars, feeling a great tightness growing in his chest. Gradually, he started to cry, the constellations blurring into watery sparkles.

When he climbed back into the room, Ron was already asleep on the bed. Louis stretched out on the floor, quiet and still, but unable to sleep for most of the night. When he eventually drifted off, his sleep was dreamless.

*****

Ron woke him roughly, with, "Take a shower, we're going to Billy's birthday party."

Louis squinted, the light from the window hitting him painfully in the eyes. "I thought we weren't going to that."

"Now we're going," said Ron, with finality, so Louis pulled himself up off the floor and out into the hall.

After showering, he borrowed some of Ron's clothes. He told Ron, "I think I got a little blood on my pants."

Ron gave him a sharp look and said, "So? Throw them out." And he held out the room's trashcan, half full, with no trash bag. Louis tossed the pants. "Keep those," Ron said, indicating the clothes Louis had put on.

"Thanks," said Louis.

In the sunlight through the window the stuff coming off of Ron looked less like smoke to Louis and more like a shadowy cloud. It was easier to see in the daytime. He didn't say anything about it. The cloud around Ron was dark, but not the black it had looked last night — more of a burnt grayish-brown. Around his own hands, Louis could see a similar darkness. When he went to fix his hair in the mirror, he could see it all around him. It looked dark, black, shaded but without color.

They went downstairs where Ron's sister, Lisa, was watching TV and reading a magazine. She was fourteen, two years younger than Louis. Something in the magazine was entertaining; she was looking at a picture and grinning with enthusiasm.

Ron said, "Hey, where's Nick."

Lisa looked up, said, "Nick went to see Andie, he probably won't be home till after supper. Mom went over to Stan's." She looked at Louis and smiled. "Hi, Louis, I like your shirt." It was really Ron's shirt. It was bright yellow and said, "Dare to Say No to Drugs" on the front.

Ron disappeared into the kitchen. Louis said to Lisa, "Thanks," and, to make conversation, "what are you reading?"

Lisa showed him the cover: *Cosmopolitan.* She giggled and said, "Hey, do guys really think like that?" She pushed the article she was reading toward him. Louis read the title, "Guys Uncensored, The Dirty Thoughts Men Have."

Louis, blushing, said, "I don't need to read that."

Lisa stopped smiling, seeming suddenly embarrassed.

"Sorry," she said.

Louis looked at her, said, "Okay let me read it," and took the magazine. But he didn't look at it; he was looking at the haze around Lisa, not nearly as dark as his or Ron's. It was a rich reddish orange, full of shadows and highlights. Lisa's hair was loose and frizzy, and there was much of it. Now Louis could see wisps of this reddish-orange color escaping from the blonde curls and around her face.

Lisa became shy under his scrutiny. Fascinated, Louis watched the color around her dim to a much softer, pastel red. "What?" asked Lisa, "What is it?" Her nose and brow wrinkled.

"I don't know," said Louis. He knew he shouldn't say anything about the colors. "You're getting really pretty." But he knew that wasn't the right thing to say, either, though it was true. All the color came vibrantly back around her, and she grinned big, and said, "You think so?" He hoped she didn't tell Ron or Nick he had called her pretty. He wanted to take it back. Instead, he said, "Yes," handing the magazine back to her without reading it.

"I just got up, I haven't even gotten ready yet," she said. Ron came back in, then, and Louis self-consciously took a step back from where Lisa sat on the couch.

"You want some pop tarts?" Ron asked Louis. "We got strawberry."

"Yeah, strawberry," said Louis, and Ron disappeared back into the kitchen.

Lisa asked, "You guys going somewhere?"

"Yeah." Louis sat down on the easy chair across from the couch. "Billy's birthday party, I guess."

"Really?" Lisa leaned forward, excited. "Can I go?" Louis shrugged. Lisa said, "I got invited, I can go, you don't mind, do you?"

Ron came back in, saying, "Lisa, shut up, no you can't go."

Lisa ignored Ron, looking at Louis as she repeated, "Please can I go?"

Louis said, "Yeah, you can go, if Ron says okay."

Ron narrowed his eyes at Louis, but said, "Okay fine. We're leaving in five minutes, we're not waiting around."

Lisa jumped up off the couch. "I have to go get ready," she said, smiling at Louis, "and take a shower and everything."

"We're not waiting around," Ron repeated.

"Louis, don't let him leave without me," Lisa said, disappearing up the stairs.

To Louis, Ron said, "Quit hitting on my sister."

"I wasn't." Lisa reappeared at the top of the stairs wearing only a towel. She walked to the upstairs bathroom, not too quickly, not looking at them. Louis looked away, back at Ron, who was frowning.

There was a dark look in Ron's eyes Louis wasn't sure he'd ever seen before. For the first time, Louis thought then of Ron as a killer. As someone who had killed. Of course Louis, too, was someone who had killed, but now he saw Ron as something different, something to fear. He believed in Ron's friendship. But the act of killing, as unintended or accidental as it had been, had revealed them, Louis recognized, as animals, and Louis doubted if they could be trusted with life, and with their own judgment of it.

131

Louis shivered and followed Ron into the kitchen. Ron handed him a glass plate with two pop tarts on it, toasted brown. He bit into one. Ron pulled a box of cereal out of a pantry and stuck his arm into it, grabbing a handful to dump into his mouth. Chewing, he said, "I didn't want to take my sister."

"I know," said Louis.

They were interrupted by the sound of the front door opening. They walked around the wall to see Nick throwing himself down on the couch.

Ron said, "I thought you had left already."

Nick looked up, and Louis could see he was sweating. "Guys, listen, it wasn't there," Nick said. He wiped at his clammy face. Then his eyes focused and he looked closely at them for the first time, at their faces, then at the pop tart in Louis' hand. During this time Louis watched the dark smoky shadows around Nick suddenly tighten, pulling in, taking on the barest hint of an orange cast.

Ron said, "What do you mean it wasn't there?" Sounding irritated. "What, you mean the body?"

"Shut up!" said Nick once, quickly, glaring suddenly at Ron. Ron turned his profile to Nick, looking toward the kitchen, clenching his jaw, just as Lisa came running down the stairs. It was obvious she could feel the tension in the room. She slowed, silent as she came down the last few steps. She had put on some jean shorts rolled tight at mid-thigh, and a pink t-shirt with a cartoon ghost that said "Spooky" right across her chest. Nick looked at her, then back at Ron. "Are you going somewhere?"

Lisa said, "We were going to Billy's birthday party."

Nick looked somehow offended. "Billy's birthday party?"

"Yeah, man," Ron said, impatiently, raising his eyebrows meaningfully as he added, "You know, we just felt like going out somewhere."

Nick shook his head. "No, no you aren't."

Louis said directly, "You told us to go somewhere."

Nick looked hard at Louis, then said, "Yes, I did." Silently, Louis handed him the pop tart. Nick took it and bit into it. He turned back to Ron and spoke while chewing. "Hey, let's go talk for a minute, okay?" He stood up and brushed by Lisa on the stairs. Ron followed, glancing at Louis as he walked by, eyebrows raised a bit, expression unreadable.

Lisa came the rest of the way down the stairs, looking quizzically at Louis. "What was that about?" She seemed mostly unconcerned with the drama between her brothers.

Louis shook his head a little and brushed it off. "Nothing, you know, Nick said something and Ron got his feelings hurt." Lisa nodded as if that explained everything. "You look nice," Louis said.

Lisa blushed and said, "Thanks, I got this shirt for two dollars at thrift town."

"It's cute," said Louis. He sat down on the couch. Lisa hesitated, then sat down next to him. Louis said, "I'm not sure we're going to Billy's birthday party after all."

"Yeah?" said Lisa.

"Yeah. I think Ron might have to stay home."

"Yeah?" said Lisa. Then, after a brief pause, "Maybe you and me can go."

Louis looked at her. "That would be fun," he said, "but I don't think it would be a good idea."

Lisa's lips tightened into a small frown as she looked

down at her feet and scratched her knee. Louis watched her, a bit overwhelmed at the way she almost looked on fire with the sun streaming through the reddish haze around her. His inexplicable visions were growing clearer and brighter, and he found himself caught between the desire to stare and the self-conscious need to look away. He was very anxious about this, ashamed of his vision - too real to be ignored - and made inarticulate by the fear of being discovered. After an awkward silence, Lisa picked up the remote to the TV and turned it on.

It was in the middle of a re-run of *The Simpsons.* Louis had seen it before, but it was entertaining and he loosened up a bit. At one point when she laughed, he felt Lisa relax into his side, leaning into him. From the corner of his eye he could see the top of her head. Little tendrils of amber smoke rose from her still damp hair, and when he breathed in the flowery aroma of her shampoo, he had the strange and fleeting idea that he was seeing the scent of her rising into the air.

He started to feel very odd and nervous. He stood up with the sudden desire to move around, excusing himself with, "I should go see what's up with Ron." At the same time, Ron and Nick started coming down the stairs. He froze, his knee still touching Lisa's knee on the couch, but neither of the two brothers were paying any attention to him. Ron's eyes were red and swollen, like he had been crying, and Nick still looked agitated and a bit confused.

All Ron said was, "We might be leaving in a little while, no rush," and went into the kitchen. Nick didn't say anything at all, or even look at them, as he too turned the corner into the kitchen.

Both were out of sight when the phone rang. Lisa was quick to pick it up, before it had even finished the first ring. "Hello?" she said, then held it by her knee as she yelled into the kitchen, "Nick, it's Pete." She put the phone back to her ear. Louis could hear Nick from the kitchen as he picked up the phone, yelling back, "I got it." Lisa kept the phone to her ear, with no intention of hanging up. Louis shook his head at her, taking the phone from her hand and returning it to the cradle. Lisa leaned back into the couch, grinning at him.

He shrugged at her, as if to say, *what's so funny*, but she just kept grinning. He could tell she was in a good mood, a fun mood, but he couldn't match it. "You don't know anything about anything," he told her.

"I know enough," she said. She turned her attention back to the TV, a slight smile still on her face. Louis turned and left her there, following Nick's voice into the kitchen.

"Bring it over here," Nick said into the phone. Louis sat down at the kitchen table, across from Ron. "Just bring it over here," Nick said again, impatiently. He hung up the phone and looked at Ron, then Louis. He stood up abruptly and walked over to the kitchen door, looking into the living room. "Lisa, go somewhere," he said. He looked back into the kitchen, at Louis. "Louis, take her somewhere, please."

"Sure," said Louis, but all the urgency and hidden anxiety was starting to give him a headache. He said, "You guys going to tell me what's going on?"

Nick, still looking out the door, said to Lisa, "Were you and Louis going somewhere?"

Ron said, "We don't know what's going on."

Lisa came into the kitchen, saying, "Are we going to that birthday party?"

Louis didn't want to go to a birthday party. To tell the truth, he wanted the quiet of his own home, which would at this time be empty. He could sense Nick's and Ron's desperate desire to fix things, to protect themselves, to cover their tracks, but he himself was feeling separated, frustrated, and he was starting to get angry. *Leave me out of your plans*, he wanted to say, *look what you've already done to me.* They all looked at him, waiting. He shook his head and said, "I'm going to walk to my house. I don't really feel up to that party."

Nick said, quickly, "You and Lisa are going to your house?"

Louis could tell Lisa didn't like that, the way Nick was trying to get rid of her. He felt a small rush of anger at Nick, at the way he was always pushing people around. Ignoring Nick, he said, "Lisa, you want to come to my house for a while?" She shrugged like it didn't matter, but Nick could see she did want to go. "Come on," he said, and left the kitchen. He went straight to the front door and out, only looking back to see if Lisa was following. Neither of them spoke anything until they had turned the corner two houses down.

"How far is your house?" asked Lisa, who had never been there.

"Not far," Louis said, giving her a little smile. She seemed to sense that he was not in the mood for chatter, merely following along beside and slightly behind him.

In the fresh air, his claustrophobia and the strange

136

sense of urgent frustration were fading. He was surprised at how comfortable their silence was, now, outside away from her house. On the other hand, he felt far from normal. His mind was full of things; he knew he could share none of them with Lisa. She was easygoing and funny. He liked her, but they didn't know each other well enough to be called friends.

After the events of the previous day, as the hazy clouds of smoke had appeared around his friends, he had called into question his own perceptions, and even to some degree his own sanity. He had been, not frightened, but certainly concerned. *My mind is playing tricks on me*, is what he thought, which meant, *It's not to be trusted.*

Now, in the daylight, he began to wonder if sanity mattered at all. Though a sense of ugliness had permeated the house they had just left, there was nothing like it in the open air. Louis had, in truth, never seen such beauty.

He slowed enough that Lisa was walking beside him. He wanted to look at her without her notice. In the sunlight, unimpeded by shadow, she glowed. Not in the metaphorical sense – well, yes, that, too – but in his own vision, with a clean, prismatic, jewel-like highlight of green surrounding her.

The whole street was lit up in the same way. There were trees along the sidewalk, each lit with its own fire. The grass in the yards and along the street, dry as it was under the summer sun, sparkled as though covered with dew.

Louis was transfixed. He slowed to a stop, taking it in. Lisa stopped too, looking at him with her head cocked to one side and her brow furrowed. Still, she didn't say anything. He wondered for a moment if she could see it the way he was seeing it, the world lit up like a giant crystal disco ball. But there was nothing in her eyes that hinted she shared his vision. She was looking at him, simply, waiting for him.

He looked up at the sky. Beads of white danced in his vision. The sun was behind him. He could feel its heat on the back of his head. He turned to look at it, with no feeling of impending danger, just simple curiosity. But it was *too* bright, *too* dazzling. For a moment he could see the sun, rainbows dancing around it, not the blazing white he was used to. Then he felt his eyes burning and watering, a pain in his head that felt like he was splitting.

The next thing he knew, he was lying on the ground with his eyes closed. He could feel Lisa beside him, holding his arm. She was saying, "Danny? Danny, are you okay?"

He opened his eyes, but to his alarm nothing changed. "I can't see," he said.

"Are you okay, Danny?" she repeated.

"Why are you calling me Danny?" he asked, that just registering. And then, the alkaline taste of fear on his tongue, "Why can't I see?" But to his relief, the darkness in his eyes began to lighten. His eyes watered, and now the black gave way to soft, great smudges of light, a bright crystal violet, and blue around it that he decided must be the sky. He blinked, trying to clear the liquid from his eyes.

"Danny?" Lisa said again.

"I'm not Danny," Louis said, his voice a tight arrow of frustration. Now his eyes were clearing. He blinked again, tears streaming down his face, and when he opened his eyes he could see Lisa in front of him. "I'm not Danny," he repeated.

She was holding tightly to his arm, and he saw her own tears with surprise. "What?" she said, "Who's Danny?"

Louis said, "You called me Danny," but she quickly shook her head.

"No, I didn't."

Louis said, "Why am I on the sidewalk?"

"You fell over," she said. "You were moving funny." He started to stand up. She grabbed his arm and pulled to help him. In a moment, he was standing again. "Are you all right?" she asked.

Louis didn't know; he didn't know what had happened. As far as he could see nothing had changed; the things of the world still glowed with eerie light. He remembered looking at the sun and felt a shiver of fear. *Is that what did it?* he wondered. He turned his back to it without looking up at it. "I'm fine," he told Lisa, and began walking again, toward his house.

"Maybe we should go back, Louis."

"I'm fine," he said again.

Lisa shook her head, refusing at first to walk with him. He shrugged and continued on down the street. She started to follow after a moment, but they had only gone a short distance when Pete's car came crawling down the street toward them. He pulled up next to them, the window down. "Louis," he said.

"Hey, Pete," Louis said. "Going to Nick's?"

Pete nodded. Lisa said, to Pete, "Pete, take Louis with you." There was a taut urgency to her voice, and Pete's eyebrows came down abruptly.

"Why?" he asked, "What did he say?" To Louis he sounded suspicious.

Lisa looked confused. "I think he had a seizure or something."

Louis shook his head. "I did not," he said, "I didn't have a seizure."

But Pete was looking at him closely, now. "You don't look too good."

"I'm fine," Louis said.

"You aren't freaking out, are you?"

"No," Louis said shortly, "I'm not freaking out."

Pete looked at him for a second, then at Lisa. "Get in the car, Louis."

Louis said, "Pete, I'm fine." He started walking toward his house again. "Come on," he said to Lisa. She followed, leaving Pete behind them, idling his engine by the side of the road.

"Louis," said Pete, "come back here."

Louis ignored him. He heard the car door open and shut. Louis didn't look back, but he could hear Pete's feet behind them, and wasn't surprised to feel a hand on his shoulder. Irritated, he looked down at Pete's hand, curling tightly onto the fabric of his t-shirt. He was wearing a ring Louis hadn't seen before (*but he had, hadn't he?*). It was silver, of a snake eating its own tail, with a single red jewel for an eye. The red jewel glared in the sun. The strange dark smoke rose from Pete's hand, but the ring itself had its own quality. Looking at it, Louis again felt his eyes watering, the splitting pain in his head. He felt himself losing his balance, Pete's hand sliding off of his shoulder as he fell forward. He held his hands out to stop his fall, but by the time they touched the ground he was no longer aware of them.

*****

He was lying on his back again, looking up into the sky. Pete was leaning over him, blocking out the sun. He looked panicked. Louis said, "You okay, Pete?"

Pete said, "Louis?"

Louis said, "Yeah, what?" At the same time he became conscious of the sound of Lisa crying.

Pete said, "What the fuck is wrong with you?" Louis started to sit up, and Pete pushed him back into the ground. "What's wrong with you, why are you shaking like that?"

Louis said, "I'm not shaking." He wasn't, as far as he could tell. But then Pete took a hold of his shirt and he *did* start to shake, but it was Pete who was shaking, not Louis.

Pete said, "Quit freaking out." He repeated it, louder, "Quit freaking out!" and then he screamed into Louis' face, "STOP FREAKING OUT!!" Spittle flew from his lips onto Louis' face, and Louis pushed him away with a sudden heave that sent Pete sprawling.

Louis stood over Pete, leaning back on his hands with a shocked look on his face. "I'm fine," Louis said. Lisa wasn't exactly crying, but her face was blotched and her hair was a bit mussed and most of her brilliant light had darkened to little tendrils of brown smoke. Louis said, again, "I'm fine," but he didn't feel fine, he felt like he was losing his mind.

141

Lisa said, "Louis, you had a seizure." He shook his head at her, a silent *no*, but instead of continuing to his house, he walked around and opened the door to the passenger side of Pete's car. He sat down, closed the door, leaned back and closed his eyes. He could hear Pete and Lisa talking, but he ignored them. He wanted his splitting headache to go away. He tried not to think. He heard Pete getting into the car, Lisa climbing into the back seat, where they had carried the body just the day before. He kept his eyes closed, resisting the temptation to look around, the insane impulse to check for blood on the seat.

When they pulled into Nick's and Ron's driveway. Louis's headache was still going strong. He opened his eyes as the car came to a stop, opened the door, got out. He said nothing to Pete or Lisa. He didn't knock on the door, he never did; he just opened it and walked in. Nick and Ron were sitting on the couch watching TV. It seemed very dark after being outside. Nick and Ron looked up from the TV, squinting toward the door. Louis ignored them and went into the kitchen. He opened the refrigerator and took out a Coke, popped the tab and drank from it. He sat down at the kitchen table. He could hear Pete now, in the other room, and Lisa, and now they were all talking, too loud. He didn't pay any attention. He shut his eyes. He tried not to think. He drank from his Coke and hoped for his head to stop splitting.

No one came in to check on him there. He didn't know what they were doing and didn't care. He was grateful, as gradually his headache faded and he felt okay to open his eyes. His head was free of pain and felt reasonably whole by the time he finished his Coke. The other room sounded empty. He got another Coke from the refrigerator and sat and drank it. The kitchen was lit coldly white by the fluorescent bulb on the ceiling. He finished the second coke and got up and left the kitchen.

The living room was as empty as it had sounded. Louis went up the stairs, to Ron's room. It too was empty, but the window was open. Louis climbed out the window and onto the roof. They were all there except Lisa: Nick, Pete, and Ron. They were arguing about something, but they stopped when Louis climbed up to join them. Though they all seemed stressed, their looks weren't at all accusatory. Ron motioned him to sit down, so he did, next to Ron, in the shade.

Nick said, "Here, look at this," handing something to him. Louis took it. It was an envelope, unmarked on the outside, with a card in it. On the front of the card it said:

BIRTHDAY DINNER

For

"Danny Glass"

July 27, 7:00pm

1506 Arquette Ct.

YOU ARE INVITED!

The name, "Danny Glass," was handwritten, and on the inside of the card was this message, written in the same hand:

Hey Pete,

I'd love it if you came to my birthday dinner on Wednesday. Bring your friends. You know the ones I mean.

Danny

Louis read it twice, then handed it back to Nick. "Who's Danny?" he asked.

"Who do you think?" Pete asked, shortly.

Ron said, "Pete found that in his dad's car this morning. Don't really know when it was put there."

Louis said, "I thought you didn't know him, Pete."

Pete said, "I don't know him, okay? He was in one of my classes, I don't think I even ever talked to him." There was an aggravated edge to Pete's voice, and Louis realized Pete was not nearly as calm as he wanted to seem.

Louis said, "This can't be from him." They all looked away as if they had no answer to that. "It can't be from him," Louis insisted again, "he's dead."

"Maybe he's not," Ron said quietly.

Louis shook his head. "No, you all saw him." But there was something about them all, especially Nick. For the first time, color rose around all of them other than black and grey. A pale yellow haze surrounded all of them, though Pete's had something of a sickly greenish cast. Ron and Nick looked calm, besides, at least more relaxed than they had since yesterday. "You guys are planning on going to this thing tonight." He was beginning to feel numb, it was all coming too fast.

Ron said, "Yeah, we already decided."

"I just want to know what's going on," Nick added.

"It's a trap," Louis said, because it didn't make any

sense any other way. "You don't really believe today is this kid's birthday, do you?"

"A trap for what?" said Ron. "From who?" And that was the thing. There was no way it made any sense.

"Someone's playing games with us," Louis said. "Look at it, someone knows what we did, we're being set up."

Nick looked at him, his mood unchanged. "You think we don't know this is some kind of set up? So what? You know it's not the police, you know it's not something they would do." He was speaking for Louis' benefit, not arguing, this Louis could already tell. It was decided. "I just want to know what's going on," said Nick again. "I've been going crazy." Louis had no reply to that, nothing to argue on that score, of course. "It's just after four now," Nick went on. "We're going to take Mom's car at around 6:30. You coming?" He already knew the answer; they all did.

"Yeah," said Louis, still shaking his head. "Yeah, might as well."

They all seemed relieved, but Louis felt none of it. When Pete said, "Smoke a blunt?" Louis waited while it was rolled, and he hit it when it came around. But he kept his eyes half-closed and imagined himself far away, separate from all of them.

*****

But he felt much less separate from them standing on the porch in front of 1506 Arquette Ct. Over the past two hours trepidation had begun eating its way into his nervous system. Louis could feel it in them all, a sweaty apprehension that caused them to avoid each other's eyes and clench their jaws shut. The weed extended the moments too long, blurring curiosity and fear into a strange sense of waiting.

He had not been to this house before, but he had passed it many times. He had always considered it something of an eyesore. In a neighborhood where a single birdbath could be considered decorative, this yard stood out for its numerous rock decorations, elaborate shrubbery, and wooden figures like ducks and pixies.

They crowded onto the small porch like trick-or-treaters, silent as Pete rang the doorbell. None of them knew what to expect. Louis tried to picture the face of the boy they had beaten to death and could not. Were that face to appear in the doorway, he wondered if he would recognize it.

But when the door opened, it was a woman who stood there. Louis did not know her, but he had seen her before, often, working in the yard. She was ugly – not grotesquely so, but too much sun over too many years had burned her skin into a blotchy brown. Of course he had not before seen the strange play of light he saw around her now, as to Louis's eyes she seemed enshrouded in a viscous inky indigo that obscured the play of her features in the shadow of the door. She was smiling, showing teeth that were possibly dentures.

"You must be Danny's friends," she said, "Please, come in."

She pulled the screen door open. Pete shrugged, the tiniest motion of the shoulders, then stepped through the door. The others followed, Louis bringing up the rear, self-consciously pushing the door closed behind him. Nick let burst an awkward cough, then said, "Is Danny around?"

146

The woman, leading them down a hallway, said, "He was getting ready, it seems he isn't done yet." She stopped when she came to a dining room, ushering them in. "I'm his Aunt November. I've wanted to have a special dinner for Danny for a long time," she said. "I'm so glad you could come." The dining room was elegantly prepared. The tablecloth was white with subtle satin trim and still showed marks from having been folded. Louis wondered if the woman could sense their anxiety. The table had not been entirely set, though silverware and napkins marked each place, and a flower arrangement stood in the center of the table.

The utter normalcy of everything made him want to scream. Danny was nowhere in sight, and Louis was unsurprised. He was convinced the boy was dead. He found the possibility of Danny's being alive somehow embarrassing, and cruelly contradictory to the heaviness he felt on his spirit.

Seated at the table, across from Louis, Nick said boldly, "So how has Danny's summer been?" No doubt he thought he seemed casual, but to Louis there was a discernible tremor in his voice. Louis looked at the strange woman, Aunt November, taking advantage of her face turned in profile, wondering what she knew, or didn't know.

"You should ask him when he joins us," the woman said, her casual tone too easy, too friendly. She made a quick gesture with her hands, palm to palm, almost like a silent, sliding clap. "Soup should be ready, coming right up," and she disappeared through a swinging door. It swung back towards them, like a pendulum, and through it Louis glimpsed a section of kitchen, dominated by a huge oven and a stove top covered with pans.

Ron said, in a quick whisper, "She's going to eat us," expelling a short bark of a laugh. Louis shot him a look, but Ron went on, less whisper and more of a taunt, "Like Hansel and Gretel. 'My, what a big oven you have, the better to fry you with.'" He started to laugh bitterly again, but Pete was suddenly snarling at him, his upper lip pulled back with such savagery that Ron flinched. Pete seemed about to say something, but instead he dropped his lip back over his teeth, and the silence stretched until Aunt November's return through the swinging door. She was still smiling as though this were a normal dinner party, carrying bowls that she deposited around the table. She disappeared back through the door.

"What about poison?" said Nick, quietly, after the door closed. "She could be trying to poison us." Ron was nodding as if he'd already thought of that.

Pete said, "I don't think she even knows," but the others looked at him like he was crazy. No one had time to reply; a second later the woman returned again, this time with a mid-size pot of soup and ladle.

"It's borscht," she said, placing the bowl in the middle of the table, next to the flower arrangement. "That's a traditional Russian beet soup. The recipe has been in our family for generations." They looked at the soup, the bright redness of it, and no one made a move to take any. November sat down at the head of the table, took the ladle and filled her own bowl. They watched her spoon a few bites into her mouth with evident pleasure. "Please," she said, when no one moved to join her, "help yourselves."

Louis was watching her with fascination. The deep

murky blue cloud around her was thickening, becoming almost completely opaque. The room, though not brightly lit, was far from dark; still, except for her eyes, her features were becoming increasingly hard to make out.

The room was too silent. Aunt November said nothing as she ate her bowl of soup. The boys wanted to demand answers, but no one quite dared.

Louis was the first to take some of the soup. He sensed the woman's smile as he started to fill his bowl. The others looked at him without expression, waiting. Too much waiting, Louis thought. Too much waiting. The soup was red like tomato soup, but thinner, and had vegetables and tiny bits of meat. It tasted delicious. The warmth of it in his mouth gave him a rush of courage. He said, to Aunt November, "How old is Danny today?" He ignored the others, each adopting their own reproving look.

Aunt November, on the other hand, smiled as though they had shared a secret joke. "He is seventeen."

Louis forced a smile of his own. He said, "I only met him once." He paused, but the woman didn't respond. He said, "He seemed nice." Only after he had spoken did he recognize the finality in his tone, and the tinge of solemnity that made Ron, across from him, look down into his empty bowl.

November still smiled, but it seemed to Louis her eyes grew colder. All she said was, "Yes, he is." Her gaze trailed off into the distance. Then she looked at him sharply, saying, "You must be Louis."

That shocked him, but he tried to keep his face clear and his voice even. "Yes, how did you know?"

Aunt November said, "Danny told me about all of you.

He was looking forward to your visit."

"Really?" Louis said, "I wasn't sure he'd remember me." The indigo blur around November darkened at this, but she sat silently, her expression unchanged. He said, "I'm sorry, we should have introduced ourselves. This is Ron," who looked up from his bowl and nodded once before looking back into his bowl. "This is Nick," who mumbled "nice to meet you" and couldn't seem to hold back a scowl, and finally, "This is Pete," who didn't look up or say anything at all.

"He is blessed to have such friends," said November, with apparent warmth. "He's always been a very quiet boy, rather like you young men seem to be." She gave them all a sweeping glance, then continued eating her soup.

Louis continued eating his as well, noticing with surprise that he had almost finished the bowl. He said to Ron, rather pointedly, "This is delicious, you should have some," which made Ron scowl and November's smile widen.

"Yes, please," said November, "you simply *must* try the borscht." When the others still didn't reach for the ladle, Aunt November grabbed it herself, scooping soup into Ron's bowl, then into Nick's, then into Pete's. Ron and Nick mumbled quiet thanks. Pete said nothing, but after a moment, all began eating the borscht.

Louis finished his bowl of borscht, and pushed it away from him. Aunt November finished hers as well, and they regarded each other across the table, the others still sullenly slurping their soup. November smiled and stood up. "I will go see what's taking Danny so long." She opened the swinging door into the kitchen and disappeared.

Immediately, Nick gave him a savage look and whispered, "Quit talking to her, Louis."

"I thought you wanted to know what the hell was going on?" Louis demanded.

Nick shook his head furiously. "She doesn't know anything, can't you see that? She's trying to get information out of us, can't you tell?" His tone was impatient and condescending. "She knows he's dead. I don't think she knows we did it."

"She knew my name," said Louis.

Ron said, "Yeah, now thanks to you she knows all our names."

Louis said, "You don't think she did already?"

Pete said, "I'm telling you, she doesn't know anything."

"Who cares?" Ron demanded. "Who cares? I'm just going to eat and get out of here, I'm tired of this shit."

At that, Pete got a strange pinched look on his face. "Why don't we just leave now?" he asked. But he didn't stand up, and neither did anyone else.

For his part, Louis's head was starting to hurt again, with that strange splitting sensation, like someone was gently sawing through the center of his forehead. He closed his eyes for a moment. When he opened them, the other three were looking at him anxiously.

"What?" he asked.

Ron said, "Are you okay, Louis?"

Louis said, "I'm fine," though his eyes were blurring some, and he had to blink a lot. He wiped at his forehead, at his eyes, and realized he was squinting.

Pete asked, "What's going on with you, Louis?"

Louis, confused, said, "What are you talking about?"

But then, the door to the kitchen swung open and Aunt November returned, carrying more bowls. Humming softly, she exchanged the bowls she was carrying for the bowls of borscht, most of them uneaten. Stacking them precariously, she exited. "Pot roast will be out in a moment," she said as the door swung shut behind her.

Immediately, Nick whispered furiously, "Shut up! All of you! She only knows what you all tell her!"

The door swung open again as Aunt November returned, with an oven mitt on one hand, the other protected by a washcloth, awkwardly carrying a large pot. Steam curled up around the glass lid where the handle of a spoon protruded. She put it in the middle of the table, dropping the mitt and washcloth next to it, then she took the lid off the pot and set it on the oven mitt.

"Our family's special pot roast," she said, a proud glint in her eye. "Traditional recipe."

It smelled delicious, similar to the microwaveable turkey potpies that were Louis's favorite, and despite – or perhaps because of – all the tension he felt a pang of hunger gnawing. Nick, impatient, said, "Miss November, is Danny coming?" Aunt November didn't respond. She took the big spoon and the bowl in front of Nick and filled it with pot roast. She did the same with Pete's, then Ron's. Nick pushed his chair back a little bit and made a small show of looking at his watch. "It really is getting late," he said, as she filled Louis's bowl.

Aunt November raised her eyebrows at that, but filled her own bowl before saying, "Really? There's a lot of food here, I'd hate to see it go to waste." She picked up a fork and took a bite, chewing assiduously, eyebrows still perked too high on her forehead. "Delicious," she said, and took another.

Nick's eyes flicked away from her and down, giving in, and he pulled his chair a little closer and picked up his own fork. With his silent permission, all the boys started eating, except Louis, who was watching with fascination the strange yellow steam that was coming off the roast. He had never seen colored steam come off food that he could remember, but the others didn't seem to notice, so he too was silent, his own eyes betraying too much color recently.

He still hadn't taken a bite, when Pete suddenly made a face and spit into his hand, saying, "I think I bit into a bone," then, looking into his hand, "that's not a bone. What is that?" They all tried to lean over to look into his hand, but it was Louis who had the best angle.

"What is that?" he asked, "is that a snake?" He could see it was, though, it was a snake eating its own tail, and he had seen it before. "Pete," he said, "isn't that your ring?"

Pete looked at him, puzzled. "This isn't a ring," he said, but Louis knew better, knew it to be a piece of a ring he had seen before.

"It's part of a ring," he said. "You were wearing that ring, I saw you."

But Pete was shaking his head firmly. "I don't wear rings," he said, "I don't like rings."

"I'm sorry, did your ring break?" interrupted Aunt November, with sympathy, "Is your mouth okay?"

"It wasn't my ring," said Pete, indignantly, but then Nick startled them all by attacking his food with a vengeance, with such wildness that Ron snorted.

"Damn, Nick," he said, "hungry?"

Nick barely slowed down. "Shut up," he said quickly, decisively, and kept attacking his bowl. The others, astonished, were silent, even Aunt November, eyebrows still raised, smiling benignly. In less than a minute, his bowl was empty. He set it down with a smack, and looked November in the eye. "Done?" he said, definitely more of a question than a statement. But after Aunt November nodded slightly, there was no hesitation as Nick pushed his chair back and left the dining room, hurrying down the hall and out of the house.

In the silence, Aunt November began humming again. The song was easy to recognize; "happy birthday to Danny, happy birthday to you."

Dully, Louis said, "Shouldn't we wait for Danny to sing happy birthday?"

"Oh, Danny," said November. "Poor Danny." She was still smiling. "Danny's at the table now."

"You're crazy," Ron said. "What is this, a séance?" But Louis knew it was more than that, and maybe Pete did too – the expression on his face was unreadable.

"You expect us to eat this?" he asked. He knew what it was, he understood now what this madwoman had done. And now he felt the borscht, or whatever had been in the soup, heavy on his stomach, and a sharp pain, a splitting pain, again through his head. His throat spasmed, and he swallowed, hard.

November was still smiling, but her eyes had taken on a cold distance. "Little boys think they can do anything," she said. "What, you don't have the stomach for it?" Her tone was contemptuous.

"You don't know me," said Louis. "You don't know anything about me." He was tired of her indigo glow, and now he could see his own spark red around his hands. Angrily, he grabbed his own fork and took a bite. He expected a lance of pain in his brow; instead, to his surprise, the pain lessened and the colors around November noticeably dimmed. He took another bite, the pain slowly evaporating. He thought wildly, *it can all go back*. Of course nothing could go back, he knew that more than ever. But bite after bite, as the tell-tale colors faded around November and his friends, he felt sanity returning. He understood that he would not be ill, that his stomach and intestines and liver and whatever else he didn't know about would do their proper job. In time whatever he put into his body this night would leave it, and the body would go on. Indigestion would pass. It always did

Louis bit. He chewed. He tasted. With difficulty, he swallowed. Eventually, his bowl clean and his vision clear, he left the table.

www.ingramcontent.com/pod-product-compliance
Lightning Source LLC
Chambersburg PA
CBHW060352180626
46817CB00008B/2980